VILLA TRISTE

Villa
Triste

PATRICK MODIANO

Translated from the French by
JOHN CULLEN

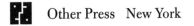 Other Press New York

Production editor: Yvonne E. Cárdenas
Text designer: Julie Fry
This book was set in Bulmer and Bell Gothic by
Alpha Design & Composition of Pittsfield, NH.

10 9 8 7 6 5 4 3 2

Library of Congress Cataloging-in-Publication Data

Names: Modiano, Patrick, 1945- | Cullen, John, 1942- translator.
Title: Villa triste / by Patrick Modiano ; translated from the French by John Cullen.
Other titles: Villa triste. English
Description: New York : Other Press, [2016] | "First published in French as Villa Triste by Editions Gallimard, Paris, in 1975."
Identifiers: LCCN 2015037068 | ISBN 978-1-59051-767-3 (paperback) | ISBN 978-1-59051-768-0 (ebook)
Subjects: LCSH: Alienation (Social psychology)—Fiction. | Identity (Psychology)—Fiction. | France—Social life and customs—20th century—Fiction.
Classification: LCC PQ2673.O3 V5713 2016 | DDC 843/.914—dc23 LC record available at http://lccn.loc.gov/2015037068

for Rudy
for Dominique
for Zina

1.

They've torn down the Hôtel Verdun. It was an odd building bordered by a rotting wooden veranda, and it stood across from the train station. Commercial travelers would stop there to sleep between two trains. It had a reputation as a hotel that rented rooms by the hour. The rotunda-shaped café next door has also disappeared. Was it called the Dials Café, or maybe the Café of the Future? In any case, now there's a big vacant space between the station and Place Albert I.

Rue Royale, on the other hand, hasn't changed a bit, but because the season is winter and the hour late, you feel like you're walking through a ghost town. You pass shop windows—the Chez Clément Marot bookstore, Horowitz the jeweler's ("Deauville, Geneva, Le Touquet"), the Fidel-Berger English pastry shop—and then, farther on, the René Pigault hairdressing salon. The Henri à la Pensée windows. Most of these luxury shops are closed during the off-season. When you reach the arcades, you can see the red and green neon lights of the Cintra shining at the end on your left. On the opposite sidewalk, at the corner of Rue Royale and Place du Pâquier, is the Taverne, once a popular meeting place for young people. Does it still have the same clientele today?

Nothing remains of the big café, with its chandeliers and mirrors and the umbrella tables that overflowed onto the pavement. Around eight o'clock in the evening, there would be people moving about from table to table and forming little groups. Bursts of laughter. Blond hair. Clinking glasses. Straw hats. From time to time, a beach robe would add a dash of bright color. Everyone was getting ready for the night's festivities.

Over there on the right is the Casino, a massive white structure open only from June to September. In the winter, local burghers play bridge twice a week in the baccarat room and the department's Rotary Club holds its meetings in the grill room. Behind the Casino, the Albigny Park slopes very gently down to the lake and its weeping willows, its bandstand, and the wharf where you can catch the dilapidated boat that shuttles from one small lakeside village to another: Veyrier, Chavoires, Saint-Jorioz, Éden-Roc, Port-Lusatz…Too much cataloging. But there are some words you have to sing to yourself over and over, tirelessly, to a lullaby tune.

You follow Avenue d'Albigny, which is lined with plane trees. It runs along the lake, and at the moment when it curves to the right, you spot a white wooden portal: the entrance to the Sporting Club. A gravel drive, with several tennis courts on either side. Beyond them — all you have to do to remember is close your eyes — the long row of bathing huts and the sandy beach, nearly three hundred meters long. In the background, an English-style garden surrounds the Sporting Club's restaurant and bar, which stands on the site of an old orangery. This all forms a peninsula, which at the turn of the twentieth century belonged to the automobile manufacturer Gordon-Gramme.

Opposite the Sporting Club, on the other side of Avenue d'Albigny, Boulevard Carabacel begins. It twists and turns up to the Hermitage, Windsor, and Alhambra hotels, or you can take the cable car. In summer it runs until midnight, and you wait for it in a little station that looks like a chalet from the outside. The vegetation here is thoroughly mixed, it's hard to tell if you're in the Alps, on the shores of the Mediterranean, or somewhere in the tropics. Umbrella pines. Mimosas. Fir trees. Palms. If you take the boulevard up the hillside, you discover the panorama: the entire lake, the Aravis mountains, and across the water, the elusive country known as Switzerland.

The Hermitage and the Windsor now house only furnished apartments. However, no one has bothered to take out the Windsor's revolving door or the sun lodge at one end of the Hermitage's lobby. Remember? It was invaded by bougainvillea. The Windsor dated from around 1910, and its white façade had the same meringue-like appearance as the façades of the Ruhl and the Négresco in Nice. The ocher-colored Hermitage was more sober and more majestic. It resembled the Royal hotel in Deauville — like a twin, actually. Have they really been converted into apartment buildings? No lights at the windows. You'd have to be brave enough to walk through the dark hallways and climb the stairs. Then maybe you'd see for yourself that nobody lives here.

As for the Alhambra, it's been razed to the ground. There's no trace of the gardens that once encircled it. Plans are surely afoot to build a modern hotel on the site. It costs me a negligible effort of memory to recall that in summer the gardens of the Hermitage, the Windsor, and the Alhambra closely corresponded to an image of the Garden of Paradise or the Promised Land. But which of the three had the immense bed of dahlias and the balustrade you leaned on to look out over the lake below? It doesn't matter. We must have been the last witnesses to that little world.

It's very late on a winter night. On the other side of the lake, you can barely make out the misty lights of Switzerland. There's nothing left of the luxuriant Carabacel vegetation but some dead trees and stunted bushes. The façades of the Windsor and the Hermitage are black, as though charred. The town has lost its cosmopolitan, summery sheen. It's dwindled into a departmental capital. A little burg, nestled in the remote French provinces. The notary and the sub-prefect play bridge in the disused Casino. So does Madame Pigault, the owner of the hairdressing salon, a blonde in her forties scented with Shocking. At her side, young Fournier, whose family owns three textile factories in Faverges. Also present is Servoz, of the Chambéry pharmaceutical laboratories, an excellent golfer. It appears that Madame Servoz, as brunette as Madame Pigault is blond, spends much of her time at the wheel of her BMW, driving between Geneva and her villa in Chavoires, and that she's quite fond of young people. She's often seen in the company of Pimpin Lavorel. And we could provide a thousand other equally vapid, equally appalling details about daily life in this little town, because people and things here have certainly not changed in twelve years.

The cafés are closed. A pink light filters under the door of the Cintra. Shall we go in and see whether the mahogany paneling has changed and the lamp with the tartan shade is in its proper place to the left of the bar? They haven't removed the photographs of Émile Allais, taken at Engelberg when he won the world skiing championship. Or those of James Couttet. Or the one of Daniel Hendrickx. They're all lined up above the rows of aperitif bottles. Of course, the photos have yellowed somewhat. And in the semidarkness, the only customer, a red-faced man wearing a checked jacket, is distractedly groping the barmaid. In the early 1960s, she had a harsh beauty, but since then she's gained weight.

You can hear the sound of your own footsteps as you walk along the deserted Rue Sommeiller. On your left, the Regent cinema is the same as it ever was: it's still got the orange roughcast façade, and REGENT is still spelled out in English-style, plum-colored letters. Nevertheless, they must have modernized the inside and changed the wooden seats and the Harcourt portraits of film stars that decorated the lobby. The station square is the only place in the town where some lights are still on and a few signs of life still visible. The Paris express is due at six minutes past midnight. Soldiers on leave from the Berthollet barracks arrive in noisy little groups, carrying their metal or cardboard suitcases. Some of the young men sing "O Christmas Tree," no doubt because the season is approaching. They cluster together on platform 2, whacking one another on the back. You'd think they were leaving for the front. Among all those military overcoats, a civilian suit, beige in color. The man who's wearing it doesn't seem to suffer from the cold; he clasps the green silk scarf around his neck with a nervous hand. He goes from group to group, turning his head left and right with a distraught expression, as if searching for a single face in all that crowd. In fact, he's just asked a soldier a question, but the young man and his two companions answer him only with derisive looks. Other soldiers turn and whistle as he passes them. He pretends to pay them no attention and nibbles on his cigarette holder. Now he's standing off to one side with a young and very blond soldier in the elite Chasseurs Alpins, the Alpine Hunters. The youngster looks embarrassed and from time to time glances furtively at his comrades. The man in the suit leans on his shoulder and whispers something in his ear. The young chasseur tries to break away. Then the man slips an envelope into the soldier's overcoat pocket, looks at him without saying anything, and as it's beginning to snow, turns up the collar of his jacket.

The man's name is René Meinthe. He abruptly raises his left hand to his forehead and leaves it there like a visor. A dozen years ago, this was a familiar gesture of his. How he's aged...

The train has pulled into the station. The soldiers storm aboard, jostle one another in the corridors, lower the windows, pass suitcases through them. Some sing "Auld Lang Syne," but the majority prefer to bellow "O Christmas Tree." It's snowing harder. Meinthe stands there unmoving, still holding up his hand like a visor. The towhead observes him through the window with a slightly cruel smile playing on his young lips. He fiddles with his uniform beret.

Meinthe waves to him. The carriages move off, carrying away their clusters of singing, waving soldiers.

With his hands thrust into his jacket pockets, he heads for the restaurant in the station. The two waiters are clearing the tables and sweeping up around them with broad, languid gestures. Behind the bar, a man in a raincoat is putting up the last glasses. Meinthe orders a cognac. The barman curtly informs him that the bar is closed. Meinthe again orders a cognac.

"In this place," the man replies, lingering on each syllable, "in this place, we don't serve fairies."

And the two waiters behind him burst into laughter. Meinthe doesn't move; he stares at a point somewhere before his eyes and looks exhausted. One of the waiters has switched off the lights on the left-hand wall. The yellowish glow around the bar is the only remaining illumination. They're waiting with folded arms. Are they going to bust his face? Or, I don't know, maybe Meinthe's going to slam his hand down on the grimy counter and declare, "I am Astrid, QUEEN OF THE BELGIANS!" posing and laughing in his old insolent way.

2.

What was I doing, at the age of eighteen, on the shore of that lake, in that fashionable spa resort? Nothing. I was living in a boardinghouse, the Lindens, on Boulevard Carabacel. I could have opted for a room in town, but I preferred to be on the high ground, steps away from the Windsor, the Hermitage, and the Alhambra, whose luxury and dense gardens reassured me.

Because I was scared to death, a sensation I've never been without; but in those days it was much more vehement, and much more irrational. I had fled Paris, convinced that the city was becoming dangerous for people like me. A disagreeable, police-heavy atmosphere prevailed there. Far too many roundups for my taste. Exploding bombs. I'd like to be precise in my chronology, and since the best reference points are provided by wars, the question is, Which war was going on then? It was the one known as the Algerian War, at the very beginning of the 1960s, a period when people drove around in Floride convertibles and women dressed badly. So did men. As for me, I was afraid, even more than I am today, and I'd chosen that place of refuge because it was five kilometers from the Swiss border. At the first sign of danger, all I had to do was cross the lake. Naïve as I was, I thought the closer you got to Switzerland, the better your chances of coming out all right. I didn't yet know that Switzerland doesn't exist.

The "season" had started on June 15. Galas and festivities would follow hard on one another. The "Ambassadors'" dinner at the Casino. Appearances by the singer Georges Ulmer. Three performances of *Listen Up, Gentlemen*. The Chavoires golf club's July 14 fireworks display, the Marquis de Cuevas ballet, and other events I'd be able to recall if I had the tourist office's printed program in my hands. I kept it, and I'm sure it's stuck in the pages of one of the books I was reading that year. But which one? The weather was "magnificent," and the regular visitors predicted sunny days all the way until October.

I very seldom went swimming. In general, I spent my days in the lobby and gardens of the Windsor, and in the end I persuaded myself that there, at least, I was safe. When I was overcome by panic—a flower that opened its petals slowly, just above my navel—I would stare out across the lake. You could see a village from the Windsor's gardens. Barely five kilometers away, straight ahead. You could swim that far. At night, in a small motorboat, the trip would take about twenty minutes. For sure. I tried to calm down. I whispered to myself, articulating each syllable: "At night, in a little motorboat…" That made everything better, and I went back to reading my novel or some innocuous magazine. (I'd forbidden myself to read newspapers or listen to radio bulletins. Every time I went to the movies, I took care to arrive after the newsreel.) No, it was best to avoid knowing anything about the fate of the world. Best not to aggravate that fear, that feeling of imminent disaster. Concentrate on trivialities: fashion, literature, cinema, variety shows. Stretch out on the long deck chairs, close your eyes, and relax. Above all, relax. Forget. Right?

Toward the end of the afternoon, I'd go down into the town. I'd sit on a bench on Avenue d'Albigny and observe all the lakeshore activity, the traffic of sailboats and paddleboats. It was comforting. The foliage of the plane trees overhead protected me. Then I'd proceed on my way, stepping slowly and cautiously. In the Taverne on Place du Pâquier, I'd always choose a table at the back of the terrace and always order a Campari and soda. And I'd contemplate all the young people around me, seeing that I was, after all, one myself. They became more and more numerous as the night went on. I can still hear their laughter, and I remember how their hair fell over their eyes. The girls wore pirate pants and gingham shorts. The boys affected blazers with crests, open-necked shirts, and scarves. Their hair was cut short in the style called *rond-point*. They were making plans for their parties. The girls attended them in tight-waisted dresses with loose, baggy skirts and ballet shoes. The young men, well behaved and romantic, would be sent to Algeria. Not me.

At eight o'clock, I went back to the Lindens for dinner. The boardinghouse, whose exterior reminded me of a hunting lodge, welcomed about a dozen regular customers each summer. They were all over sixty, and my presence irritated them at first. But I breathed with great discretion. By means of scanty gestures, deliberately lifeless eyes, and a set face—blinking as little as possible—I strove to avoid aggravating an already precarious situation. They recognized my goodwill, and I think that in the end they looked on me more favorably.

We took our meals in a rustic Savoy-style dining room. I could have conversed with my nearest neighbors, a dapper elderly couple from Paris, but certain hints suggested that the man was a former police inspector. The other tables were also occupied by couples, except for a gentleman with a thin mustache and a spaniel face who gave the impression of having been abandoned there. From time to time, through the hubbub of conversations, I could hear his hiccups, brief outbursts like barks. The guests would move into the lounge and sigh as they sat down on the cretonne-covered armchairs. Madame Buffaz, the proprietress of the Lindens, would serve herbal tea or some after-dinner drink. The women would talk among themselves. The dog-faced gentleman, sitting off to one side, would sadly light a Havana cigar and observe the game.

I would have gladly remained among them, in the soft, soothing light of lamps with salmon-pink silk shades, but I would have had to talk to them or play canasta. Would they have allowed me to stay, I wonder, if I had just sat there unspeaking and watched them? I went back down into the town. At exactly nine fifteen—right after the newsreel—I entered the Regent cinema, or sometimes I chose the Casino, where the theater was more elegant and more comfortable. I've found one of the Regent's old schedules for that summer:

Tendre et violente Elisabeth by H. Decoin	June 15–17
Last Year at Marienbad by Alain Resnais	June 24–30
The Black Chapel by R. Habib	July 1–8
Testament of Orpheus by J. Cocteau	July 9–16
Captain Fracasse by P. Gaspard-Huit	July 17–24
Qui êtes-vous, M. Sorge? by Y. Ciampi	July 25 – Aug. 2
La Notte by M. Antonioni	August 3–10
The World of Suzie Wong by R. Quine	August 11–18
Le Cercle vicieux by M. Pécas	August 19–26
Le Bois des amants by C. Autant-Lara	Aug. 27 – Sept. 3

I'd really love to see some reels from those old films.

After the movie, I'd go back to the Taverne and drink another Campari. By that time, midnight, the young people had deserted it. They must have been dancing somewhere else. I contemplated all those chairs, those empty tables, and the waiters who were taking in the umbrellas. I stared at the big illuminated fountain on the other side of the square, in front of the entrance to the Casino. It changed color constantly. I amused myself by counting how many times it turned green. As good a pastime as any, don't you think? Once, twice, three times. When my count reached fifty-three, I'd get up, but mostly I didn't even bother to play that game. I'd go off into a dream, taking mechanical sips of my drink. Do you remember Lisbon during the war? All those guys slumping in the bars and lobby of the Aviz Hotel, with their suitcases and their steamer trunks, waiting for an ocean liner that never came? Well, twenty years later, I had a feeling I was one of those guys.

On the rare occasions when I wore my flannel suit and my only tie (an American had given it to me; it was navy blue, decorated with fleurs-de-lis, and sewn on the back was a label with the words "International Bar Fly." I would later learn that this was a secret society for alcoholics. Thanks to that tie, they could recognize one another and perform small services if needed), I might step into the Casino and stand on the threshold of the Brummel Lounge, watching the people dance. They were generally between thirty and sixty years old, but sometimes a younger girl could be seen among them, in the company of a tall, slim fiftyish man. The clientele was international and rather stylish, and they'd be swaying to popular Italian hits or Jamaican calypso tunes. Later I'd go upstairs to the gaming rooms. Often enough, someone would win a serious jackpot. The most extravagant players came from quite nearby in Switzerland. I remember a very stiff Egyptian with glossy red hair and gazelle eyes who would pensively stroke his English officer's mustache with one forefinger. He played with five-million-franc gaming plaques and was said to be King Farouk's cousin.

I'd be relieved to find myself in the open air. I would go back to Carabacel, walking slowly along Avenue d'Albigny. I've never known nights so lovely, so crystal clear as those were. The sparkling lights of the lakeside villas dazzled me, and I sensed something musical in them, like a saxophone or trumpet solo. I could also perceive the very soft, immaterial rustling of the plane trees on the avenue. I'd wait for the last cable car, sitting on the iron bench in the chalet. The room was lit only by a night-light, and I'd let myself slip into that purplish semidarkness with a feeling of total confidence. What was there for me to fear? The noise of war, the din of the world would have had to pass through a wall of cotton wool to reach this holiday oasis. And who would have ever thought of coming to look for me among these distinguished summer vacationers?

I got off at the first stop, Saint-Charles-Carabacel, and the now empty cable car continued its climb. It looked like a big, shiny worm.

Back at the Lindens, I'd take off my moccasins and tiptoe down the hall, because old folks are light sleepers.

3.

She was sitting in the lobby of the Hermitage, settled on one of the big sofas in the back and not taking her eyes off the revolving door, as if waiting for someone. My armchair was only two or three meters away, and I could see her profile.

Auburn hair. Green shantung dress. And the stiletto-heeled shoes women wore. White.

A dog lay at her feet. From time to time, he yawned and stretched. He was a huge, lethargic Great Dane. He had a white coat with black patches. Green, red, white, black. The combination of colors affected me with a kind of numbness. How did I wind up next to her on the sofa? Did the Great Dane perhaps serve as a go-between, lumbering up to me lazily so he could sniff me?

I noticed that she had green eyes and very light freckles, and that she was a little older than me.

That same morning, we walked in the hotel gardens. The dog led the way. We followed him along a path that ran under a canopy of clematis with big blue and purple flowers. I pushed aside hanging clusters of laburnum; we skirted lawns and privet hedges. There were, if I recall correctly, some rock plants of various frosty hues, some pink hawthorn blossoms, a flight of steps bordered with empty basins. And the immense bed of yellow, red, and white dahlias. We leaned on the balustrade and looked at the lake below us.

I've never been given to know exactly what she thought of me in the course of that first encounter. Maybe she took me for a bored rich boy, some millionaire's son. In any case, what amused her was the monocle I wore on my left eye to read, not out of foppishness or affectation but because my vision was very much worse in that eye than in the other.

We're not talking. I can hear the whisper of water from a sprinkler in the middle of the nearest lawn. Someone's coming toward us down the stairs, a man whose pale yellow suit I spotted from some distance away. He waves to us. He's wearing sunglasses and wiping his brow. She introduces him to me as René Meinthe. He corrects her at once: "Doctor Meinthe," stressing both syllables of the word "doctor." And he smiles, but with a grimace. It's my turn to introduce myself: Victor Chmara. That's the name I used on the registration form at the Lindens.

"You're a friend of Yvonne's?"

She answers that she's just met me in the lobby of the Hermitage, and that I use a monocle to read. This obviously amuses her no end. She asks me to put on my monocle to show Dr. Meinthe. I comply. "Very good," says Meinthe, nodding and looking pensive.

So her name was Yvonne. And her family name? I've forgotten it. I conclude that twelve years suffice for you to forget the legal name of people who have mattered in your life. It was a pleasant name, very French, something like: Coudreuse, Jacquet, Lebon, Mouraille, Vincent, Gerbault…

At first sight, René Meinthe seemed older than we were. Around thirty. Medium height. He had a round, nervous face and wore his blond hair combed back.

We returned to the hotel through a part of the garden I wasn't familiar with. The gravel paths were rectilinear, the lawns symmetrical and laid out in picturesque English style. Around each of them were flamboyant beds of begonias or geraniums. And here as well, there was the soft, reassuring whisper of the sprinklers. I thought about the Tuileries of my childhood. Meinthe proposed that we have a drink and then go to lunch at the Sporting Club.

They seemed to find my presence natural, and you would have sworn we'd known one another for years. She smiled at me. We talked about trivial things. They asked me no questions, but the dog laid his head on my knee and examined me.

She stood up and announced she was going to her room to get a scarf. So she lived in the Hermitage? What was she doing here? Meinthe took out a cigarette holder and nibbled at it. That was when I began to notice he had a great many tics. At long intervals, the muscles in his left cheek tensed, as if he were trying to catch a slipping, invisible monocle, but his dark glasses hid much of this twitching. Occasionally he'd thrust out his chin as though provoking someone. And then his right arm was shaken from time to time by an electrical discharge that communicated itself to his hand, which would trace arabesques in the air. All these tics were coordinated most harmoniously, and they gave Meinthe an agitated elegance.

"You're on vacation?"

I replied that I was. And I said I was lucky the weather was so "splendid." And I found this holiday resort a "paradise."

"Is this the first time you've come here? You didn't know the area before?"

I heard a touch of irony in his voice and took the liberty of asking him in my turn if he himself was here on vacation. He hesitated. "Oh, not exactly. But I've known this place for years..." Stretching out his arm nonchalantly, he indicated a point on the horizon and said in a weary voice, "The mountains...The lake...The lake..."

He took off his dark glasses and gave me a sad and gentle look. He was smiling. "Yvonne is a marvelous girl," he told me. "Mar-vel-ous."

She was walking back to our table with a green chiffon scarf tied around her neck. She smiled at me and then never took her eyes off me. Something expanded in the left side of my chest, and I decided I was having the best day of my life.

We climbed into Meinthe's car, an old cream-colored Dodge convertible. All three of us sat in front, with Meinthe at the wheel, Yvonne in the middle, and the dog on the backseat. Meinthe stamped violently on the gas pedal, and the Dodge skidded on the gravel, barely missing the gateway of the hotel. We drove slowly along Boulevard Carabacel. I couldn't hear the engine anymore. Had Meinthe switched it off so we could coast down? The umbrella pines on either side of the road blocked the sun's rays and cast patterns of light and shadow. Meinthe was whistling, I abandoned myself to the car's gentle swaying, and Yvonne's head rested on my shoulder every time we went around a curve.

At the Sporting Club, we were the only diners in the restaurant, the former orangery shaded from the sun by a weeping willow and some large rhododendron bushes. Meinthe explained to Yvonne that he had to go to Geneva and would come back that evening. I thought they might be brother and sister. But no. They didn't look at all alike.

A group of about a dozen people arrived and chose the table next to ours. They'd come from the beach. The women wore colored terry cloth sailor shirts, and the men had on swim robes. One of them was taller and more athletic than the others, with wavy blond hair. He made a remark to no one in particular. Meinthe took off his dark glasses. He was suddenly quite pale. He pointed at the tall blond man and spoke in a very high-pitched voice, practically a squeal: "Look, there's that tramp Carlton. The biggest SUH-LUTT in Haute-Savoie…"

The man pretended not to hear, but his friends turned toward us openmouthed.

"Did you understand what I said, Miss Carlton?"

For several seconds there was absolute silence in the dining room. The athletic blond man lowered his head. His companions were petrified. Yvonne, on the other hand, didn't bat an eye, as if accustomed to incidents of this sort.

"Have no fear," Meinthe whispered, leaning toward me. "It's nothing, nothing at all…"

His face had become smooth, childlike; all his tics were gone. Our conversation resumed, and he asked Yvonne what she'd like him to bring back for her from Geneva. Chocolates? Turkish cigarettes?

He left us at the entrance to the Sporting Club, saying we could meet again at the hotel around nine o'clock that evening. He and Yvonne spoke of a certain Madeja (or Madeya), who was giving a party in a lakeside villa.

"You'll come with us, won't you?" Meinthe asked me.

I watched him walk over to the Dodge as though propelled by a succession of electric shocks. He drove off the way he'd done the first time, his wheels spinning in the gravel, and once again the automobile just missed the gate before disappearing. He raised his arm and waved to us without turning his head.

I was alone with Yvonne. She suggested a stroll in the Casino gardens. The dog walked ahead of us, more and more wearily. Sometimes he sat down in the middle of the path and we had to call out his name, "Oswald," before he'd consent to go on. She explained that it was not laziness but melancholy that made him so lackadaisical. He belonged to a very rare strain of Great Danes, all of them congenitally afflicted by sadness and the ennui of life. Some of them even committed suicide. I wanted to know why she'd chosen a dog with such a gloomy nature.

"Because they're more elegant than the others," she replied sharply.

I immediately thought about the Habsburgs, whose royal family had included some delicate, hypochondriac creatures like the dog. This was attributed to intermarrying,

PATRICK MODIANO

and their depressive character became known as "the Portuguese melancholy."

"That dog," said I, "is suffering from the Portuguese melancholy." But she didn't hear me.

We'd reached the wharf. About ten passengers were boarding the *Amiral-Guisand*. Then the gangway was drawn up. Some children leaned out over the rail, waving and shouting. The boat moved off, and it had a dilapidated, colonial charm.

"We'll have to take that boat one afternoon," Yvonne said. "It would be fun, don't you think so?"

She'd just addressed me with the familiar *tu* for the first time, and she'd spoken with inexplicable urgency. Who was she? I didn't dare ask her that.

We walked on Avenue d'Albigny, shaded by the plane trees' leafy branches. We were alone. The dog was about twenty meters ahead of us. His habitual languor was gone, and he marched along proudly, head up, abruptly veering off from time to time and performing some quadrille figures, like a carousel horse.

We sat down and waited for the cable car. She laid her head on my shoulder, and I was seized by the same giddiness I'd felt when we drove down Boulevard Carabacel in Meinthe's Dodge. I could still hear her saying, "One afternoon…we'll take…boat…fun, don't you think so?" in her indefinable accent, which I thought might be Hungarian, English, or Savoyard. As the cable car slowly climbed up, the vegetation on either side of the track looked thicker and thicker. It was going to bury us. The flowering bushes pressed against the glass panels of the funicular, and sometimes a rose or a privet branch was carried off by our passage.

In her room at the Hermitage, the window was half open, and I could hear the regular plunk of tennis balls and the players' distant cries. If there still existed some nice, reassuring idiots who wore white outfits and whacked balls over a net, then that meant the world was continuing to turn and we had a few hours' respite.

Her skin was sprinkled with very faint freckles. There was fighting in Algeria, apparently.

Night came. And Meinthe was waiting for us in the lobby. He wore a white linen suit with a turquoise scarf impeccably knotted around his neck. He'd brought some cigarettes from Geneva and insisted we should give them a try. But we didn't have a moment to lose — he said — or we'd be late for Madeja's (or Madeya's) party.

This time we zoomed down Boulevard Carabacel at top speed. Meinthe, his cigarette holder dangling from his lips, accelerated into the curves, and I don't know by what miracle we reached Avenue d'Albigny safe and sound. I turned to Yvonne, and I was surprised to see that there was not the slightest expression of fear on her face. I'd even heard her laugh once when the car swerved.

Who was this Madeja (or Madeya) person whose party we were going to? Meinthe told me he was an Austrian filmmaker. He'd just finished shooting a film in these parts — in La Clusaz, to be specific, a ski resort twenty kilometers away — and Yvonne had played a part in it. My heart beat faster.

"You're in the movies?" I asked her.

She laughed.

"Yvonne is going to be a very great actress," Meinthe declared, trampling the accelerator pedal to the floor.

Was he serious? A *movie actress*? Maybe I'd already seen her picture in *Cinémonde*, or in the cinema year-book I'd discovered in the depths of an old bookstore in Geneva, the book I would page through during my nights of insomnia. In the end, I knew the names and addresses of the actors and "technicians." Some of them remain in my memory:

JUNIE ASTOR: Photograph by Bernard and Vauclair. 1 Rue Buenos-Ayres, Paris VII.

SABINE GUY: Photograph by Teddy Piaz. Comedy — Song — Dance. Films: *Les Clandestins...The Babes Make the Law...Miss Catastrophe...La Polka des menottes... Hi Doc...*etc.

GORDINE (SACHA FILMS): 19 Rue Spontini, Paris XVI. KLE. 77–94. M. Sacha Gordine, MGR.

Did Yvonne have a "movie name" I might know? When I asked her that, she murmured, "It's a secret," and placed a finger on her lips.

Meinthe added, with a distressingly high, thin laugh, "You understand, she's here incognito."

We followed the lakeshore road. Meinthe slowed and switched on the radio. The air was warm, and we slipped through that limpid, satiny night, like no night I've ever known since, except in the Egypt or Florida of my dreams. The dog had set his chin in the hollow of my shoulder, and his breath was scorching me. The gardens to our right sloped down to the lake. Past Chavoires, the road was lined with palms and umbrella pines.

We passed the village of Veyrier-du-Lac and turned onto a steep uphill road. The front entrance of the villa stood below the level of the road. An inscription on a wooden panel named the place: THE LINDENS (the same name as my hotel). A fairly wide gravel drive, bordered by trees and a mass of neglected vegetation, led to the very threshold of the villa, a big white building in the style of Napoleon III, with pink shutters. A few cars were parked close together. We crossed the hall and stepped into what must have been the salon. There, in the filtered light of two or three lamps, I made out about ten people, some standing near the windows and others lolling on a white sofa, which was apparently the only piece of furniture. They were filling their glasses and carrying on animated conversations in German and French. A tune came from a record player on the floor, a slow melody accompanying a singer who kept repeating, in a very deep voice,

Oh, Bionda Girl...
Oh, Bionda Girl...
Bionda Girl...

Yvonne took my arm. Meinthe cast rapid glances all around, as if looking for someone, but no member of that gathering paid us the slightest attention. We stepped through a French window onto a veranda with a green wooden balustrade. There were some deck chairs and wicker armchairs. A Chinese lantern cast complicated shadows, making patterns like lace or tracery, and it was as though Yvonne's and Meinthe's faces were suddenly covered with veils.

In the garden below us, several people were crowding around a buffet table laden with things to eat. A very tall, very blond man waved and came toward us, supporting himself on a cane. His linen shirt—natural-colored, mostly open—looked like a safari jacket, and I thought about certain characters one used to meet in the colonies in the old days, the ones who had a "past." Meinthe introduced the tall man: Rolf Madeja, "the director." He leaned down to kiss Yvonne and put his hand on Meinthe's shoulder. He called him "Menthe," mint, with an accent that sounded more English than German. He led us toward the buffet, and the blond woman as tall as he was, the vague-eyed Valkyrie (she stared at us without seeing us, or maybe she was contemplating something she saw through us), turned out to be his wife.

Yvonne and I left Meinthe in the company of a young man with a mountain climber's physique and moved from group to group. She kissed everybody, and if anyone asked who I was, she said, "A friend." If I understood correctly, most of the people present had played some part in "the film." They wandered off across the garden. The bright moonlight lit up everything. We followed the grass-covered paths and came upon a cedar tree of terrifying size. When we reached the garden wall, we could hear the lapping of the lake on the other side, and we stayed there for a long moment. From where we were, you could see the house standing in the midst of the neglected grounds, and its presence surprised us as much as if we'd just arrived in the old South American city where a rococo opera house, a cathedral, and some mansions of Carrara marble are said to exist to this day, entombed by the virgin forest.

The other guests haven't ventured as far as we have, except for two or three barely distinguishable couples who are taking advantage of the dense coppices and the night. Everyone else has stayed near the house or on the terrace. We rejoin them. Where's Meinthe? Inside, maybe, in the salon. Madeja comes up to us and reveals, in his half-English, half-German accent, that he would happily stay here another two weeks, but he must go to Rome. He'll rent the villa again in September, he says, "When the film's final cut is ready." He takes Yvonne by the waist — I don't know whether he's groping her or displaying fatherly affection — and declares, "She's a very fine actress."

He stares at me, and I notice his eyes look misted, and the mist is growing denser.

"Your name is Chmara, isn't it?"

The mist has suddenly vanished; his blue-gray eyes glint. "Chmara," he says. "That's it, isn't it?"

I answer him with a tight-lipped "yes," and then his eyes grow soft again, mist over, practically liquefy. I don't doubt he has the power to regulate their intensity at will, the way you adjust binoculars. When he wants to withdraw into himself, his eyes mist over, and then the outside world is nothing but a blurred mass. I know this method well, as I often practice it myself.

"There was a Chmara in Berlin, in the old days…" he said to me. "Wasn't there, Ilse?"

His wife, lying on a deck chair at the other end of the veranda and chatting with two young people, swiveled her head toward us with a smile on her lips.

"Wasn't there, Ilse? Wasn't there a Chmara in the old days in Berlin?"

She looked at him and kept smiling. Then she turned her head and resumed her conversation. Madeja shrugged and gripped his cane tightly with both hands.

"Yes…yes…This Chmara lived on the Kaiserallee… You don't believe me, do you?"

He stood up, caressed Yvonne's face, and walked over to the green wooden balustrade. He remained there, looming, massive, contemplating the moonlit garden.

Yvonne and I sat on two poufs, side by side, and she laid her head on my shoulder. A young brunette whose low-cut bodice displayed her breasts (at every even slightly abrupt movement, they surged up out of her décolletage) handed us two glasses filled with pink liquid. She guffawed and kissed Yvonne and begged us to try the cocktail, which she'd prepared "especially" for us. If I remember right, her name was Daisy Marchi, and Yvonne told me she played the lead role in "the film." She too was going to have a great career. She was well known in Rome. Soon she left us, laughing even harder and shaking her long hair, and went to join a fiftyish man with a slender figure and a pockmarked face who was standing, glass in hand, at an open French window. He was a Dutchman named Harry Dressel, one of the actors in "the film." Other people were sitting in the wicker armchairs or leaning on the balustrade. Some women were gathered around Madeja's wife, who continued to smile, vacant eyed. Through the French window came a murmur of conversations, along with slow, syrupy music, but this time the singer with the deep voice was repeating different words:

Abat-jour
Che soffondi la luce blu...

Madeja himself was pacing up and down the lawn in the company of a little bald man who came up to his waist, so that he had to bend down to talk to him. They passed and repassed the terrace, Madeja more and more ponderous and bowed down, his companion more and more stretched and straining upward, on the tips of his toes. He emitted a buzz like a hornet, and the only words he spoke in human language were, "Va bene Rolf...Va bene Rolf...Va bene Rolf...Vabenerolf..." Yvonne's dog sat sphinxlike at the edge of the terrace and followed their comings and goings, turning his head from right to left, from left to right.

Where were we? Deep in the heart of Haute-Savoie. But however much I repeat this reassuring phrase, "deep in the heart of Haute-Savoie," I keep thinking of a colonial country, or one of the Caribbean islands. How else to explain that soft, corroding light, the midnight blue that turned eyes, skin, dresses, and alpaca suits phosphorescent? Those people were all surrounded by some mysterious electricity, and every time they made a move, you braced yourself for a short circuit. Their names — some of them have remained in my memory, and I regret not having written them all down at the time; I could have recited them at night before falling asleep, not knowing who their owners were, the sound of them would have been enough — their names brought to mind the little cosmopolitan societies of free ports and foreign bars: Gay Orloff, Percy Lippitt, Osvaldo Valenti, Ilse Korber, Roland Witt von Nidda, Geneviève Bouchet, Geza Pellemont, François Brunhardt...What's become of them? Having summoned them to this rendezvous, what can I say to them? Already in those days — soon to be thirteen years ago — they gave me the impression that they'd long since burned out their lives. I watched them, I listened to them talking under the Chinese lantern that dappled their faces and the women's shoulders. I assigned each of them a past that dovetailed with those of the others, and I wished they'd tell me everything: when did Percy Lippitt and Gay Orloff meet for the first time? Did one of them know Osvaldo Valenti? Which of them had put Madeja together with Geneviève Bouchet and François Brunhardt? Which of the other six had introduced Roland Witt von Nidda into their circle? (And I'm mentioning only those whose names I remember.) So many enigmas presupposed an infinity of combinations, a spider's web they'd been spinning for ten or twenty years.

It was late, and we were looking for Meinthe. He was neither in the garden nor on the terrace nor in the salon. The Dodge had disappeared. We ran into Madeja, accompanied by a girl with very short blond hair, on the front steps, and he reported that "Menthe" had just left with

"Fritzi Trenker," and that he was most certainly not coming back. He burst into loud laughter, surprising me, and placed his hand on the girl's shoulder.

"The staff of my old age," he declared. "You understand me, Chmara?"

Then, abruptly, he turned his back on us and went down the hall, leaning on the girl's shoulder more heavily than before. He looked like a blind ex-boxer.

That was the moment when things took a new direction. The lamps in the salon were switched off. The only light left was the night-light on the mantelpiece, whose pink glow was absorbed by great swaths of shadow. The Italian singer's deep tones had been replaced by a woman's voice, which broke and hoarsened so much you couldn't tell anymore whether you were listening to dying moans or grunts of pleasure. Then all at once the voice became pure. It intoned the same words, sweetly repeating them.

Madeja's wife is lying across the sofa, and one of the young people from the group that surrounded her on the terrace bends over her and slowly begins to unbutton her blouse. She stares at the ceiling, her lips parted. Some couples are dancing, a little too close, their movements a little too precise. In passing, I notice that the strange Harry Dressel is stroking Daisy Marchi's thighs with a heavy hand. A little group near the French window turn their attention to a spectacle: a woman doing a solo dance. She takes off her dress, her slip, her brassiere. Out of sheer idleness, Yvonne and I have joined the group. Roland Witt von Nidda, his features distorted, devours the dancer with his eyes. She's down to her stockings and her garter belt, nothing else, and she keeps on dancing. On his knees, he tries to tear off her garters with his teeth, but she dodges him every time. Finally she decides to remove her remaining accessories herself and then continues to dance, stark naked, whirling around Witt von Nidda, brushing against him, while he remains motionless, impassive, his chin thrust out, his torso arched, a grotesque matador. His twisted shadow spreads over the wall, and the woman's shadow — immeasurably enlarged — sweeps across the floor. Soon, throughout the entire house, there's nothing but a ballet of shadows pursuing one another, climbing and descending stairs, bursting into laughter, uttering furtive cries.

A corner office adjoining the salon. Its furniture included a massive desk with numerous drawers, the sort of thing I imagine could be found in the old Ministry of the Colonies, and a big dark green leather armchair. We took refuge in that office. I glanced back at the salon, and I can still see Madame Madeja's thrown-back head (her neck was resting on the arm of the sofa). Her long blond hair hung down to the floor, and you would have thought that head of hers had just been lopped off. She started moaning. There was another face, very close, whose features I could barely make out. Her groans grew louder and louder, her cries more and more unhinged: "Kill me…Kill me…Kill me…Kill me…" Yes, I remember all that.

The floor of the office was covered with a very thick wool rug, and we lay down on it. A ray of light beside us painted a grayish-blue bar that ran from one end of the room to the other. One of the windows was partly open, and I could hear the rustling of a tree whose branches rubbed against the glass. The shadow of those branches covered the book-case with a netting of night and moon. The shelves held all the volumes in the crime fiction collection *Le Masque.*

The dog fell asleep in front of the door. No more sounds, no more voices reached our ears from the salon. Had every-one else left the villa, and were we the only ones still there? A scent of old leather hung in the air of the office, and I wondered who had arranged the books on those shelves. Whose were they? Who came in here of an evening to smoke a pipe, or work, or read one of the novels, or listen to the murmuring of the leaves?

Her skin had taken on an opalescent tint. A leaf's shadow drew a tattoo on her shoulder. Sometimes it fell on her face, and you would have thought she was masked. The shadow shifted lower and gagged her mouth. I could have wished the sun would never rise so that I could stay with her there, huddled together in the depths of that silence, in that aquarium light. A little before dawn, I heard a door slam, hurried footsteps above us, and the crash of an over-turned piece of furniture. And then some bursts of laugh-ter. Yvonne had gone to sleep. The big dog lay dreaming. At regular intervals, he gave out a muffled groan. I half opened the door. There was nobody in the salon. The night-light was still on, but the glow it cast seemed dimmer, no lon-ger pink but a very delicate green. I headed for the veranda to get some fresh air. Nobody there either, under the still-glowing Chinese lantern. It swung in the wind, and sorrow-ful shapes, some of them human in appearance, scurried across the walls. Down below, the garden. I tried to identify the fragrance that emanated from that vegetation and rose to the terrace. But yes — I hesitate to say it, because the setting was Haute-Savoie — but yes: I was inhaling the scent of jasmine.

I crossed the salon again. The night-light diffused its pale green illumination in slow waves. I thought of the sea, and of the iced mint-and-lemonade drink popular on hot days: diabolo menthe. I could still hear bursts of laughter, and I was struck by their purity. They came from very far away and then suddenly got closer. I couldn't manage to locate their source. The laughter became more and more crystalline and volatile. She was asleep, her cheek resting on her outstretched right arm. The bluish bar of moonlight that lay across the room lit up the corners of her mouth, her neck, her left buttock, and one heel. On her back, the light was like a long, narrow scarf. I held my breath.

I can still see the leaves swaying outside the window and that body cut in two by a moonbeam. Why is it that a vanished city, prewar Berlin, is superimposed in my memory on the Haute-Savoie countryside that surrounded us? Maybe because she was "acting" in a "film" by "Rolf Madeja." I made some inquiries about him later, and I learned that he'd started out as a very young man in the UFA studios in Berlin. In February '45 he began work on his first film, *Confettis für zwei*, a very vapid and very gay Viennese operetta whose scenes he shot between Allied air raids. The film remained unfinished. For my part, when I call that night to mind, I'm walking past the massive town houses of Berlin as it once was, I go along quays and boulevards that no longer exist. I walk straight on from Alexanderplatz, cross the Lustgarten and the Spree. Night is falling on the four rows of linden and chestnut trees and on the passing trams. They're empty. The lights tremble. And you, you're waiting for me in that green cage shining at the end of the avenue, the winter garden of the Adlon Hotel.

4.

Meinthe stared attentively at the raincoated man who'd been putting away glasses. The man eventually lowered his eyes and returned to his work. But Meinthe remained in front of him, standing rigid, a mock soldier. Then he turned to the two others, who were watching him with nasty smiles on their faces, their chins propped on their broom handles. Their physical resemblance was striking: the same crew-cut blond hair, the same little mustache, the same protruding blue eyes. One was leaning over to the right and the other to the left, their poses so symmetrical you might have thought they were the same person, reflected in a mirror. That illusion must have occurred to Meinthe, because he walked over to the two men, slowly, frowning. When he got to within a few centimeters, he moved around to examine them from the back, in three-quarter profile, and from the side. The two men didn't move, but you could tell they were on the verge of springing into action and crushing Meinthe under a hail of fists. Meinthe stepped away from them and retreated toward the exit of the café, walking backward and never taking his eyes off them. They remained where they were, petrified under the grudging and yellowish light shed by the wall lamp.

Now he's crossing the station square, his coat collar turned up, his left hand clutching his scarf as if he's suffered a neck wound. There's a scanty snowfall. The flakes are so light and so thin that they float in the air. He turns into Rue Sommeiller and stops in front of the Regent. They're showing a very old film called *La Dolce Vita*. Meinthe takes shelter under the movie theater's awning and inspects the stills from the film, one by one, as he takes a cigarette holder out of his jacket pocket. He clamps the holder between his teeth and rummages through all his other pockets in search — no doubt — of a Camel. But there's no cigarette to be found, and then his face is convulsed by tics, the same ones as before — the twitching in his left cheek, the thrusting of his chin — but slower and more painful now than they were a dozen years ago.

He seems hesitant about which way to go: should he cross over and take Rue Vaugelas, which runs into Rue Royale, or should he continue on down Rue Sommeiller? A little below him, on the right, is the green-and-red sign of the Cintra. Meinthe stares at it, eyes asquint. CINTRA. The snowflakes swirling around those six letters turn green and red too. Green, the color of absinthe. Campari red...

He walks toward the oasis with arched back and stiff legs, and if he didn't tense himself this way, he'd certainly slip and fall on the sidewalk, a disjointed puppet.

The customer in the checked jacket is still there, but he's no longer hitting on the barmaid. He's sitting at a table in the back, beating time with his index finger and repeating, in a tiny voice that could be a very old woman's: "And zim...Boom-boom...And zim...Boom-boom..." As for the barmaid, she's reading a magazine. Meinthe hoists himself onto one of the stools and puts a hand on her forearm. "A light port, my dear," he whispers.

5.

I left the Lindens and moved into the Hermitage with her.

One evening they came to get me, she and Meinthe. I'd just finished dinner, and I was waiting in the lounge, sitting quite close to the man with the sad spaniel's face. The others were getting started on their canasta game. The women chatted with Madame Buffaz. Meinthe stopped in the doorway. He was wearing a very pale pink suit, and a dark green handkerchief bloomed from his breast pocket.

The company turned toward him.

"Ladies…gentlemen," Meinthe murmured, bowing slightly. Then he walked over to me, stiffened, and said, "We'll be waiting for you. You can have your baggage brought down."

Madame Buffaz asked me sharply, "Are you leaving us?"

I lowered my eyes.

"It had to happen sooner or later, Madame," Meinthe answered, in a tone that brooked no opposition.

"But he could at least have given us some advance notice."

I realized the woman was suddenly filled with hatred for me and wouldn't have hesitated to turn me over to the police on the slightest pretext. The thought made me sad.

"Madame," Meinthe replied to her, "there's nothing this young man can do, he's just received orders signed by the Queen of the Belgians." They all stared at us aghast, clutching their cards in their hands. My usual neighbors in the dining room examined me with an air of simultaneous surprise and disgust, as if they'd just noticed that I didn't belong to the human race.

The allusion to the Queen of the Belgians had been received with a general murmur, and when Meinthe — no doubt wishing to stand up to Madame Buffaz, who was facing him with her arms crossed — repeated what he'd said, coming down hard on every syllable: "Do you understand me, Madame? THE QUEEN OF THE BELGIANS," the murmur swelled and gave me a twinge in my heart. Then Meinthe stamped his heel on the floor, thrust his chin forward, and blurted out very rapidly, rushing the words: "I haven't told you everything, Madame…*I* am THE QUEEN OF THE BELGIANS…"

There were cries and gestures of indignation. Most of the boarders got to their feet and formed a hostile group in front of us. Madame Buffaz took a step forward, and I was afraid she'd slap Meinthe, or she'd slap me. I found this last possibility quite natural; I was, I felt, the only person responsible.

I would have liked to apologize to those people, or to wave a magic wand and make them forget what had just happened. All my efforts to pass unnoticed and hide in a safe place had been reduced to futility in a few seconds. I didn't even cast a last glance around the lounge, where the after-dinner gatherings had been so soothing for a troubled heart like mine. And I blamed Meinthe, for a brief moment. Why cause such consternation among these small-time pensioners, these canasta players? They were reassuring to me. In their company I risked nothing.

Madame Buffaz would have happily spat venom in our faces. Her lips got thinner and thinner. I forgive her. I'd betrayed her, in a sense. I'd shaken up the precious clockwork that was the Lindens. If she's reading this (which I doubt, and anyway, the Lindens no longer exists), I'd like her to know that I wasn't a bad boy at heart.

We had to bring down my "baggage," which I'd packed that afternoon. It consisted of a wardrobe trunk and three big suitcases. They contained a few clothes, all my books, my old telephone directories, and issues of *Match*, *Ciné-monde*, *Music-hall*, *Détective*, and *Noir et blanc* from the past several years. It was all very heavy. When Meinthe tried to move the wardrobe trunk, it nearly crushed him. By dint of incredible efforts, we managed to tip it over and lay it on its side. After that, we spent twenty minutes dragging it down the hall to the landing. We were bent in half, Meinthe in the front, me behind, both gasping for air. Meinthe lay down at full length on the floor, arms flung out, eyes closed. I went back to my room and as best I could, staggering all the way, I carried the three suitcases to the top of the stairs.

The light went out. I groped for the switch, but flicking it was useless; the hall remained as dark as before. On the floor below, some vague brightness filtered through the partly open door of the lounge. I could see a head poking through the opening: Madame Buffaz's head, I was almost sure. I realized immediately she must have removed one of the fuses so that we'd have to get the bags downstairs in the dark. And that realization made me start giggling nervously.

We pushed the wardrobe trunk until half of it hung out over the lower stairs and it was balanced precariously on the landing. Clutching the banister, Meinthe gave the trunk a furious kick, whereupon it slid down the stairs, bouncing off every one and making a frightful racket. You would have thought the staircase was about to collapse. Madame Buffaz's head was once again silhouetted in the crack of the lounge door, surrounded by two or three others. I heard her shriek, "Will you look at these bastards…" Someone was repeatedly hissing the word "Police." I picked up a suitcase in each hand and started down the stairs. I couldn't see a thing. Besides, I preferred to close my eyes and count under my breath to get my courage up. One, two, three. One, two, three…If I tripped, the suitcases would drag me all the way down and the impact would knock me out. There could be no stopping or resting. My collarbone was about to crack. And that horrible giggling took hold of me again.

The light came back on and blinded me. I found myself on the ground floor, in a daze but still on my feet, between the two suitcases and the trunk. Meinthe followed me with the third suitcase in his hand (it was lighter than the others because it contained only my toilet things), and I would have really liked to know what had given me the strength to get that far alive. Madame Buffaz handed me the bill, which I paid with averted eyes. Then she went into the lounge and slammed the door behind her. Meinthe leaned against the wardrobe trunk, rolled-up handkerchief in hand, patting his forehead with the precise little gestures of a woman powdering her face.

"We must go on, my boy," he said, pointing at my baggage. "Must go on…"

We hauled the wardrobe trunk to the steps outside. The Dodge was parked near the Lindens's gate, and I could make out what looked like Yvonne's silhouette in the front seat. She was smoking a cigarette, and then she waved at us. Somehow or another we managed to hoist the trunk onto the backseat. Meinthe collapsed against the steering wheel while I went to fetch the three suitcases from the entrance hall of the hotel.

Someone was standing stiffly at the reception desk: the man with the spaniel face. He took a few steps toward me and stopped. I knew he wanted to say something, but the words wouldn't come out. I thought he was going to resort to that baying sound he made, the soft, prolonged moaning I was doubtless the sole person to hear (the other pensioners at the Lindens would go on with their canasta game or their chitchat). He remained where he was, frowning, his mouth half open, making increasingly violent efforts to speak. Or was he nauseated and heaving, unable to vomit? He bent forward, practically choking. After a few minutes, he regained his composure and said in a hollow voice, "You're leaving just in time. Goodbye, Monsieur."

He held out his hand. He was wearing a rough tweed jacket and cuffed beige linen trousers. I admired his shoes: grayish suede, with very, very thick crepe soles. I was certain I'd met this man before I ever lodged at the Lindens, it must have been about ten years before. And suddenly... Yes, yes, they were the same shoes, and the man holding out his hand to me was the same one who'd so fascinated me as a child. He used to come to the Tuileries every Thursday and Sunday with a miniature boat (a faithful reproduction of the *Kon-Tiki*) and watch it float across the pond, changing his observation post, using a stick to push the boat away when it ran aground on the stone rim of the pond, checking the condition of a mast or a sail. Sometimes a group of children and even a few grown-ups gathered to observe this activity, and he'd glance at them furtively as though mistrusting their reactions. When someone asked him about the boat, his mumbled reply was yes, it was a very long, very complicated piece of work, building a *Kon-Tiki*, and as he spoke, he'd caress his toy. Around seven in the evening, he'd pick up his boat and sit on a bench to dry it with a terry cloth towel. Then he'd walk away in the direction of Rue de Rivoli, his *Kon-Tiki* under his arm. Later I must often have thought about that silhouette, moving off into the twilight.

Should I remind him of our meetings? But he'd surely lost his boat. I said, "Goodbye, Monsieur," in my turn, took hold of the first two suitcases, and slowly crossed the garden. He walked beside me in silence. Yvonne was sitting on the Dodge's front fender. Meinthe was at the wheel with his head resting on the back of the seat and his eyes closed. I loaded the two suitcases into the trunk. The spaniel-faced man watched all my movements with avid interest. When I crossed the garden again, he went ahead of me, turning around from time to time to make sure I was still there. He snatched up the last suitcase and said, "Allow me."

It was the heaviest of the three, the one with the phone books. He put it down every five meters to catch his breath. Every time I made a move to pick it up myself, he said, "Please, Monsieur…"

He was adamant about wrestling it onto the backseat by himself. He succeeded with difficulty, and then he just stayed there. His arms were hanging limply, his face a little flushed. He paid no attention to Yvonne and Meinthe. He was looking more and more like a spaniel.

"Well then, Monsieur…" he murmured. "I wish you good luck."

Meinthe drove off slowly. Before the car reached the first curve, I turned around and looked back. He was standing in the middle of the road, very close to a street-light that lit up his rough tweed jacket and his cuffed beige pants. All he was missing, in short, was the *Kon-Tiki* under his arm. There are some mysterious persons — always the same ones — who stand like sentinels at every crossroads in your life.

6.

At the Hermitage, she had not only a bedroom but also a living room, whose furniture included three armchairs covered with some printed fabric, a round mahogany table, and a sofa. The wallpaper in the living room and bedroom reproduced Toile de Jouy patterns. I had my wardrobe trunk placed in a corner of the room, standing upright so that the things in the drawers were within easy reach. Sweaters or old newspapers. I myself pushed the suitcases to the far end of the bathroom. I didn't open them, because you have to be ready to leave at a moment's notice and should consider any room you wind up in a temporary refuge.

Besides, where could I have put my clothes, my books, and my telephone directories? Her dresses and shoes filled every closet, and some were lying around on the chairs and sofa in the living room. The mahogany table was cluttered with beauty products. A film actress's hotel room, I thought. The kind of disorder journalists described in *Ciné Mondial* and *Stars*. Reading all those magazines had made a strong impression on me. And I was dreaming. I therefore avoided making overly abrupt movements and asking overly precise questions so that I wouldn't have to wake up.

It was on the very first evening, I think, that she asked me to read the script of the Rolf Madeja film she'd just played a part in. I was very touched. The movie, *Liebesbriefe auf der Berg* (Love Letters from the Mountain), is the story of a ski instructor named Kurt Weiss. In the winter, he gives skiing lessons to rich foreign women, guests at an elegant holiday resort in the Austrian state of Vorarlberg. Thanks to his tanned skin and his great physical beauty, he seduces them all. But eventually he falls madly in love with one of them, Lena, the wife of a Hungarian industrialist, and she requites his feelings. They go dancing until two in the morning at the resort's very "chic" bar, before the other women's envious eyes. Then Kurtie and Lena end the night in the Bauhaus Hotel. They swear eternal love and talk about their future life in an isolated mountain cabin. She must go back to Budapest, but she promises to return as soon as possible. "Now the screen fills with images of snow falling, followed by singing waterfalls and trees covered with young leaves. It's spring, and soon summer will come." Kurt Weiss is practicing his real profession — he's a bricklayer — and it's hard to recognize in him the handsome, bronzed ski instructor of the previous winter. Every afternoon he writes a letter to Lena and waits in vain for a reply. A local girl visits him from time to time. They take long walks together. She loves him, but he never stops thinking of Lena. After various twists and turns I've forgotten, the memory of Lena gradually fades, to be replaced in Kurtie's heart by the young girl (this was the role Yvonne played), as he comes to realize that no one has the right to ignore such tender devotion. In the final scene, they kiss against a background of mountains at sunset.

The portrait of a winter sports resort, of its habitués and their lifestyle, struck me as very well "painted." As for the young woman played by Yvonne, it was "an excellent part for a beginner."

I told her my opinion. She listened to me with great attention. That made me proud. I asked her when the film would be in the theaters. Not before September, but in two weeks Madeja would no doubt have a preliminary projection in Rome "to run through the rushes." In that case, she'd take me with her, because she really wanted to know what I thought of her "interpretation."

Yes, when I try to recall the first period of our "life together," I can hear, as though on a worn-out tape, our conversations regarding her "career." I want her to find me interesting. I flatter her…"This film of Madeja's is very important for you, but now you're going to have to find someone who really knows how to showcase your talents…Some boy genius…A Jew, for instance…" She listens more and more attentively. "You think so?" "Yes, yes, I'm sure of it."

The innocence in her face astonishes me, and I'm all of eighteen, myself. "You really think so?" she asks again. And all around us, the room grows more and more disorderly. I don't believe we went out for two days.

Where did she come from? I quickly determined she didn't live in Paris. She talked about it like a city she barely knew. She'd stayed two or three times, all of them brief, at the Windsor-Reynolds, a hotel on Rue Beaujon I remembered well. It was where my father, before his strange disappearance, used to meet me (there's a blank spot in my memory: was it in the lobby of the Windsor-Reynolds or in the lobby of the Lutetia that I saw him for the last time?). Apart from the Windsor-Reynolds, all she remembered of Paris was Rue du Colonel-Moll and Boulevard Beauséjour, where she had some "friends" (I didn't dare ask what sort). By contrast, Geneva and Milan often came up in her conversation. She'd worked in Milan, and in Geneva too. But what kind of work?

I checked her passport on the sly. Nationality: French. Domicile: 6 *bis*, Place Dorcière, Geneva. Why? To my great amazement, she'd been born in Haute-Savoie, in the very town we were in. Coincidence? Or did she actually have roots in these parts? Did she still have family here? I ventured an indirect question on this subject, but she wanted to keep something hidden from me. She answered very vaguely, telling me she'd been raised abroad. I didn't insist. In time, I thought, I would know everything.

She questioned me too. Was I here on holiday? For how long? She'd guessed right away, she said, that I came from Paris. I declared that I was taking a rest for several months at the insistence of "my family" (and I felt a visceral delight when I said "my family"), on account of my precarious health. As I provided her with these explanations, I saw a group of about ten very serious persons sitting around a table in a paneled room: the "family council" that was going to make some decisions about me. The windows of the room overlooked Place Malesherbes, and I belonged to the old Jewish bourgeoisie that had settled in Plaine-Monceau around 1890. She asked me pointblank: "Chmara's a Russian name—are you Russian?" Then other things came to mind: we lived, my grandmother and I, in a ground-floor apartment near the Étoile, on Rue Lord-Byron, to be exact, or Rue de Bassano (I need precise details). We survived by selling our "family jewels," or by depositing them in a pawnshop on Rue Pierre-Charron. Yes, I was Russian, and my title was Count Chmara. She looked impressed.

For a few days, I was no longer afraid of anything or anyone. And then the fear came back. The old shooting pain.

The first afternoon we left the hotel, we took the boat, the *Amiral-Guisand*, which made the circuit of the lake. She was wearing big sunglasses with impenetrable silvered lenses. You could see your reflection in them as though in a mirror.

The boat putted along lazily, and it took at least twenty minutes to cross the lake to Saint-Jorioz. The bright sun made me blink. I could hear the distant rumble of motorboats, the shouts and laughter of bathers. A light airplane passed overhead, pretty high up, towing a streamer on which I read the following mysterious words: COUPE HOULIGANT. Houligant Cup…? After a very long maneuver, we landed — or rather, the *Amiral-Guisard* banged against the wharf. Three or four people came on board, among them a priest dressed in a bright red cassock, and the boat resumed its wheezy cruise. From Saint-Jorioz it went to a village named Voirens. Then there would be Port-Lusatz and, a little farther on, Switzerland. But the boat would turn in time and head for the other side of the lake.

The wind was blowing strands of her hair across her forehead. She asked me would she be a countess if we got married. She spoke in a joking tone, but underneath it I could sense great curiosity. I told her she'd be called "Countess Yvonne Chmara."

"But is that really Russian, Chmara?"

"Georgian," I said. "Georgian…"

When the boat stopped at Veyrier-du-Lac, I recognized, in the distance, Madeja's white-and-pink villa. Yvonne was looking in the same direction. About ten young people took up positions on the deck beside us. Most of them were wearing tennis outfits, and the girls' fat thighs showed under their pleated white skirts. They all talked with the toothy accent cultivated around Ranelagh and Avenue Bugeaud. And I wondered why those sons and daughters of French polite society had, on the one hand, mild cases of acne, and on the other, a few too many kilos. The cause was surely their diet.

Two members of the group were debating the relative merits of Pancho Gonzales and Spalding tennis rackets. The more voluble of the two wore a goatee and a shirt decorated with a little green crocodile. Technical conversation. Incomprehensible words. A soft, soothing hum in the sunlight. One of the blond girls seemed not insensible to the charms of a dark-haired young man wearing moccasins and a blazer with a crest who was doing his best to shine in front of her. The other blonde declared that "the big party" was "not tomorrow night but the next," and that her parents "would let them have the villa." The sound of the water against the hull. The airplane came back over us, and I read the strange streamer again: COUPE HOULIGANT. They were all going (if I understood them correctly) to the tennis club in Menthon-Saint-Bernard. Their parents must own lakeside villas. And how about us, where were we going? And our parents, who were they? Did Yvonne come from a "good family," like our neighbors? And me? In any case, my title of count was quite another thing than a little green crocodile, lost on a white shirt..."Will Count Victor Chmara please come to the telephone?" Yes, that made a fine sound, like a clash of cymbals.

We got off the boat at Menthon with the others. They walked ahead of us, carrying their rackets. We went along a road lined with villas whose exteriors evoked mountain chalets and where several generations of dreamy bourgeois had been coming to spend their vacations. Sometimes the houses were hidden by clusters of hawthorn or fir trees. Villa Primevère, Villa Edelweiss, Les Chamois, Chalet Marie-Rose...The others turned left on a road that led to the wire netting surrounding a tennis court. The buzz of their talk and their laughter faded away.

The two of us turned right. A sign said GRAND HÔTEL DE MENTHON. A private road mounted a very steep slope to a graveled esplanade. From there you had a view that was just as vast as, but sadder than, the one from the terraces of the Hermitage. On this side, the shores of the lake looked deserted. The hotel was very old. In the lobby, some green plants, some rattan chairs, some big sofas covered with plaid fabric. Families would come here in July and August. The same names would recur on the register, double names, very French: Sergent-Delval, Hattier-Morel, Paquier-Panhard...And when we took a room, I thought "Count Victor Chmara" was going to stand out like a greasy stain.

Around us, some children, their parents, and their grandparents, all of them very dignified, were getting ready to leave for the beach, carrying bags filled with cushions and towels. Several young people gathered around a tall man with very short dark hair and a khaki army shirt open over his chest. He was leaning on crutches as the others asked him questions.

A corner room. One of the windows overlooked the esplanade and the lake; the other was blocked up. A cheval glass and a little table covered with a lace doily. A brass bed. We stayed there until nightfall.

As we walked through the lobby, I saw them in the dining room, having their evening meal. They were all dressed in street clothes. Even the children had on ties or little dresses. And we two were the only passengers on the deck of the *Amiral-Guisand.* The exhausted old tub chugged back across the lake even more slowly than on the trip out. It stopped at deserted wharves and then resumed its cruise. The lights of the villas sparkled through the greenery. In the distance, the Casino, floodlit and gleaming. Some party was surely going on there that night. I would have liked the boat to stop in the middle of the lake or next to one of the half-collapsed barges. Yvonne had fallen asleep.

We often dined with Meinthe at the Sporting Club. Outdoor tables, covered with white tablecloths. On each, a double-shaded lamp. You know the photograph from the children's charity ball supper in Cannes on August 22, 1939, and the other one, the one I always have on me (my father's in it, in the midst of an entire society that has vanished), taken on July 11, 1948, at the Cairo Casino the night the young Englishwoman named Kay Owen was elected "Miss Bathing Beauty"? Well, those two photographs could have been taken at the Sporting Club that year, when we used to have dinner there. Same décor. Same "blue" night. Same people. Yes, I recognized some faces.

Every time we dined together, Meinthe wore a dinner jacket of a different color and Yvonne a muslin or crepe dress. She was fond of boleros and scarves. I was condemned to my single flannel suit and my International Bar Fly tie. The first few times, Meinthe took us to the Sainte-Rose, a lakeside nightclub located past Menthon-Saint-Bernard, in Voirens, to be exact. He knew the manager, a fellow named Pulli, who he told me was an illegal resident. But this Pulli, a paunchy man with velvety eyes, seemed to be sweetness personified. He had a lisp. The Sainte-Rose was a very "chic" place. You could find the same rich summer vacationers there as at the Sporting Club. You danced on a terrace that featured a pergola. I remember holding Yvonne close to me and thinking I could never do without the smell of her skin and her hair, and the band was playing "Tuxedo Junction."

All in all, we were meant to meet and hit it off.

We'd get back very late, and the dog would be asleep in the living room. Ever since I'd moved into the Hermitage with Yvonne, his melancholy had grown worse. Every two or three hours—as regular as a metronome—he'd make a tour of the bedroom and then go lie down again. Before going back to the living room, he'd stop for a few minutes in front of our bedroom window and sit down, ears pricked, maybe following the progress of the *Amiral-Guisand* across the lake or contemplating the scenery. I was struck by the animal's sad discretion and touched to observe him performing his guard duties.

She'd put on a beach robe with big orange and green stripes and lie across the bed to smoke a cigarette. On her night table, along with a lipstick or an atomizer, there were always wads of banknotes lying around. Where did that money come from? How long had she been staying at the Hermitage? "They" had put her up there for the duration of the film. But now that it was finished? It was very important to her — she explained — to spend the "season" in this resort town. The "season" was going to be "very brilliant." "Resort," "season," "very brilliant," "Count Chmara" — who was lying to whom in this foreign language?

But maybe she just needed company? I showed myself attentive, considerate, tactful, and passionate, as one is at eighteen. On those first evenings, when we weren't discussing her "career," she'd ask me to read her a page or two of André Maurois's *History of England*. Every time I started to read, the Great Dane would immediately appear in the doorway to the living room, sit, and gravely regard me. Yvonne, lounging in her beach robe and frowning slightly, would listen. I never understood why she, who had never read anything in her life, liked that historical work so much. When I asked, she gave me vague answers: "It's very good, you know"; "André Maurois is a very great writer." I believe she'd found the *History of England* in the lobby of the Hermitage, and I think the volume became a sort of talisman for her, a lucky charm. From time to time, she'd tell me, "Don't read so fast," or ask me the meaning of a sentence. She wanted to learn the *History of England* by heart. I assured her André Maurois would be glad to know that. So then she started asking me questions about the author. I explained that Maurois was a very gentle Jewish novelist much interested in female psychology. One evening she asked me to write him a note: "Monsieur André Maurois, I am an admirer of yours. I am reading your *History of England*, and I would love to have your autograph. Respectfully, Yvonne X."

He never responded. Why not?

How long had she known Meinthe? Forever. He too—it appeared—had an apartment in Geneva, and they were practically inseparable. Meinthe practiced, "more or less," medicine. In the pages of the Maurois book, I found a visiting card engraved with these three words: "Doctor René Meinthe," and on the bathroom shelf, among the beauty products, a prescription from "Doctor R. C. Meinthe" for sleeping pills.

Furthermore, every morning when we woke up we'd find a letter from Meinthe under the door. I've kept a few of those letters; time has not dissipated their vetiver scent. I wondered where that fragrance came from. From the envelope, from the paper, or, you never know, from the ink Meinthe used? Here's one letter, chosen at random: "Will I have the pleasure of seeing you two this evening? I must spend this afternoon in Geneva. I shall telephone you at the hotel around nine o'clock. With love, your René M." And another: "Forgive me for not having given you any signs of life, but I haven't left my room for forty-eight hours. It occurred to me that in three weeks I shall be twenty-seven years old. And that I shall be a very old, very old person. I'll see you very soon. Love from your godmother, René." And this one, addressed to Yvonne in a more nervous hand: "Do you know who I just saw in the lobby? That prick François Maulaz. And he wanted to shake my hand. No, no, never. Never. He can drop dead!" (the last word underlined four times). There were many other letters.

The two of them often talked about people I didn't know. I recall a few names: Claude Brun, Paulo Hervieu, a certain "Rosy," Jean-Pierre Pessoz, Pierre Fournier, François Maulaz, "Miss Carlton," and someone called Doudou Hendrickx, whom Meinthe qualified as a "swine." I quickly realized that they were locals, that they all originally came from the town we were in, a summer vacation spot doomed to turn back into a boring little burg at the end of every October. Meinthe said that Brun and Hervieu had "gone up" to Paris, that Rosy had taken over her father's hotel in La Clusaz, and that "that prick" Maulaz, the bookseller's son, carried on openly every summer at the Sporting Club with a member of the Comédie-Française. All those people must have been their friends since childhood or adolescence. Whenever I asked a question, Meinthe and Yvonne would act evasive and interrupt their private conversation. Then I remembered what I'd learned from Yvonne's passport and imagined each of them at the age of fifteen or sixteen, in the winter, leaving the Regent cinema.

7.

If I could find one of the tourist information office's programs — white cover and, in green, the Casino and the silhouette of a woman drawn in the style of Jean-Gabriel Domergue — I could read the list of festivities and their exact dates, and that would give me some reference points.

One evening we went to see Georges Ulmer, who was singing at the Sporting Club. I believe this happened at the beginning of July, and it must have been five or six days after I'd moved in with Yvonne. Meinthe went with us. Ulmer wore a very creamy light blue suit I couldn't take my eyes off of. That velvety blue had a hypnotic power over me, so much so that I nearly fell asleep staring at it.

Meinthe suggested we have a drink. In the semidarkness, surrounded by dancing people, I heard them talk about the Houligant Cup for the first time. I remembered the light airplane and its enigmatic streamer. Yvonne was concerned about the Houligant Cup. It was the prize in a sort of concours d'elegance. According to Meinthe, you had to own a luxury automobile to take part in the competition. Would they use the Dodge, or would they rent a car in Geneva? (It was Meinthe who raised this question.) Yvonne wanted to try her luck. The jury was composed of various well-known personalities: the president of the Chavoires golf club and his wife; the president of the tourist information office; Haute-Savoie's sub-prefect; André de Fouquières (I jumped when I heard that name and asked Meinthe to repeat it: yes, it was indeed André de Fouquières, long known as "the arbiter of elegance," whose interesting memoirs I'd read); Monsieur and Madame Sandoz, the managers of the Windsor Hotel; the former skiing champion Daniel Hendrickx, owner of very chic sports shops in Megève and l'Alpe d'Huez (the man Meinthe called a "swine"); a film director whose name has escaped me (something like Gamonge or Gamace); and, finally, the dancer José Torres.

Meinthe too was excited about the contest, delighted by the prospect of competing for the Cup as Yvonne's gallant cavalier. His role would be limited to driving the car up the Sporting Club's long gravel drive and stopping in front of the jury. Then he was to get out and open Yvonne's door for her. The Great Dane would naturally be part of the show.

Meinthe assumed an air of mystery and, with a wink, handed me an envelope: the list of contestants for the Cup. He and Yvonne were the last couple entered, number 32. "Doctor R. C. Meinthe and Mademoiselle Yvonne Jacquet" (her family name has just come back to me). The Houligant Cup was awarded on the same date each year for "beauty and elegance." The organizers of the contest managed to create a fair amount of hype for their event, so much so that—as Meinthe explained to me—it sometimes got mentioned in the Paris newspapers. According to him, taking part in it would be an excellent career move for Yvonne.

And when we got up from the table to dance, she couldn't stop asking me what I thought: should she, yes or no, compete for the Cup? A serious problem. There was confusion in her look. I saw Meinthe sitting there alone with his "light" port. He was shading his eyes with his left hand. Could he possibly be crying? Now and then he and Yvonne seemed vulnerable and disoriented (disoriented is the exact word).

But of course she had to take part in the Houligant Cup. Of course. It was important for her career. With a little luck, she'd be Miss Houligant. Indeed she would. Besides, they had all started off that way.

Meinthe decided to use the Dodge. If he got it polished the day before the contest, it was still capable of making a positive impression. The beige convertible hood was practically new.

As the days passed and Sunday July 9 got closer and closer, Yvonne showed ever-increasing signs of nervousness. She knocked over glasses, she couldn't sit still, she spoke harshly to the dog. And in return he would give her a look both merciful and mild.

Meinthe and I tried to reassure her. Competing for the Cup would certainly be less demanding than making the movie. Five little minutes. A few steps in front of the jury. Nothing else. And, should she lose, the consolation of knowing that among all the contestants, she was the only one who'd already acted in a film. A professional, in a way.

We ought not to be unprepared, Meinthe opined, and he proposed a dress rehearsal on Friday afternoon, on a wide, shaded avenue behind the Alhambra Hotel. I sat on a garden chair and represented the jury. The Dodge slowly moved forward. Yvonne fixed her lips in a strained smile. Meinthe drove with his right hand. The dog turned his back to them and remained immobile, like a figurehead on a ship.

Meinthe pulled up directly in front of me and, bracing his left hand on the car door, sprang vigorously over it. He landed elegantly, legs together, back straight. He dipped his head, sketching a bow, walked around the Dodge with neat little steps, and deftly opened Yvonne's door. She got out, holding the dog tightly by the collar, and took a few timid steps. The Great Dane cast his eyes down. They got back in the car, and Meinthe leaped over the driver's door again, regaining his post behind the wheel. I admired his agility.

He was determined to repeat this act in front of the jury. Couldn't wait to see the look on Doudou Hendrickx's face.

The evening before, Yvonne wanted to drink champagne. Then she slept restlessly. She was the little girl on the day of the school pageant, almost in tears before stepping up onto the stage.

Meinthe had made a morning appointment with us: in the lobby, ten o'clock sharp. The Cup was scheduled to begin at noon, but he needed some time beforehand to see to certain details: general inspection of the Dodge, various instructions for Yvonne, and maybe also some stretching exercises.

He insisted on being present at Yvonne's final preparations. When she hesitated between a fuchsia turban and a big straw hat, he cut her off impatiently: "The turban, my dear, the turban." She'd chosen a white linen coat dress. Meinthe was wearing a sand-colored shantung suit. I've got a good memory for clothes.

We went out into the sun, Yvonne, Meinthe, the dog, and I. I've never known such a July morning, either before or since. A light breeze stirred the big flag flying from the top of a mast in front of the hotel. Blue and gold. What country's colors were those?

We coasted down Boulevard Carabacel.

The other contestants' cars were already parked on both sides of the very wide drive that led to the Sporting Club. Upon hearing their names and numbers called out over a loudspeaker, the couples had to present themselves at once before the members of the jury, who were installed on the restaurant terrace. As the drive ended in a rotary below them, they would be looking down on the proceedings.

Meinthe had ordered me to place myself as close as possible to the jury and to observe the competition for the Cup in meticulous detail. I was to pay particular attention to Doudou Hendrickx's face when Meinthe performed his acrobatic routine. If necessary, I could jot down some notes.

We sat in the Dodge and waited. Yvonne virtually glued her forehead to the rearview mirror and checked her makeup. Meinthe had donned some strange steel-rimmed sunglasses and was patting his chin and temples with his handkerchief. I stroked the dog, who turned upon each of us, one by one, a look of desolation. We were parked alongside a tennis court where four players — two men and two women — were engaged in a match, and in an attempt to distract Yvonne, I pointed out that one of the men resembled the French comic actor Fernandel. "What if it's him?" I suggested. But Yvonne didn't hear me. Her hands were shaking. Meinthe concealed his anxiety behind a little cough. He turned on the radio, which drowned out the monotonous and exasperating sound of the tennis balls. We stayed there unmoving, the three of us, our hearts beating, as we listened to a news bulletin. Finally, the loudspeaker announced, "Will the contestants for this year's Houligant Elegance Cup please make themselves ready." Then, two or three minutes later: "Couple number 1, Madame and Monsieur Jean Hatmer!" Meinthe grimaced nervously. I kissed Yvonne and wished her good luck, and then I took an alternate path to the Sporting Club restaurant. I was feeling pretty emotional myself.

The jury was seated behind a row of white wooden tables, each adorned with a green-and-red parasol. A great press of spectators crowded around. Some were lucky enough to be sitting down and drinking aperitifs; others remained on their feet, dressed in their beach attire. In accordance with Meinthe's wishes, I slipped through the throng and got as close to the judges as I could, close enough to spy on them.

I immediately recognized André de Fouquières, whose photographs I'd seen on the covers of his works (my father's favorite books, which he'd recommended to me, and which had given me great pleasure). Fouquières wore a Panama hat with a navy blue silk band. His chin rested on the palm of his right hand, and his face expressed elegant weariness. He was bored. At his age, all these summer holidaymakers in their bikinis and their leopard-skin swimsuits looked like so many Martians. Nobody here to talk to about Émilienne d'Alençon or La Gándara. Except for me, had the occasion arisen.

The man in his fifties with the leonine head, blond hair (did he dye it?), and suntanned skin: Doudou Hendrickx, for sure. Talking nonstop to his neighbors, laughing loudly. He had blue eyes and emitted an aura of healthy, dynamic vulgarity. A woman, a brunette very bourgeois in appearance, was smiling knowingly at him: the Chavoires golf club president's wife, or the tourist office president's wife? Madame Sandoz? Gamange (or Gamonge), the cinema man — that must have been the guy with the tortoise-shell glasses and the business suit: gray with narrow white stripes, double-breasted jacket. If I make an effort, a personage of about fifty, with wavy gray-blue hair and a greedy mouth, appears before me. He kept his nose in the air, and his chin too, doubtless wishing to look energetic and supervise everything. The sub-prefect? Monsieur Sandoz? And what about José Torres, the dancer? No, he hadn't come.

Already a garnet-red Peugeot 203 convertible was proceeding up the drive. It came to a halt in the middle of the rotary, and out stepped a woman wearing a puffy dress and carrying a miniature poodle in one arm. The man remained behind the wheel. The woman took a few steps in front of the jury. She was wearing black shoes with stiletto heels. A peroxide blonde of the type supposedly preferred by ex-King Farouk of Egypt, about whom my father had spoken so often and whose hand he claimed to have kissed. The man with wavy gray-blue hair announced "Madame Jean

Hatmer" in a toothy voice, molding each syllable of the name. She let go her miniature poodle, which landed on its paws, and began to walk, trying to imitate runway models in fashion shows: eyes vacant, head afloat. Then she got back into the Peugeot. Feeble applause. Her husband had a crew cut. I noticed how tense his face was. He backed up and executed a deft U-turn; you could tell he considered it a point of honor to drive as well as possible. He must have polished his Peugeot himself, to make it shine so bright. I decided they were a young married couple, the man an engineer from a respectable upper-middle-class family, the woman of humbler origins, both good at sports. And following my habit of setting everything somewhere, I imagined them living in a "cozy" little apartment on Rue du Docteur Blanche, in Auteuil.

Other contestants followed in their turn. Alas, I've forgotten all but a few of them. The thirtyish Eurasian woman, for example, with her fat, red-haired escort. They were in an aqua-green Nash convertible. When she got out of the car, she took one robotic step toward the jury and then stopped. She was seized with nervous trembling. Her panic-stricken eyes darted all around her, but she didn't move her head. The big redhead in the Nash called to her: "Monique…Monique…Monique…" and it sounded like a lament, an entreaty meant to soothe an exotic and mistrustful animal. He too got out of the car and took her by the hand. He pushed her gently down onto her seat. She burst into tears. Then they roared away, wheels spinning in the gravel, nearly sideswiping the jury when they turned. They were followed by a nice sexagenarian couple whose names

I remember: Jackie and Tounette Roland-Michel. They drove up in a gray Studebaker and presented themselves to the judges together. Tall and red haired with an energetic, equine face, she was dressed in tennis clothes. He was of medium stature, with a little mustache, a substantial nose, a mocking smile, and the physique of a real Frenchman as imagined by a Californian film producer. An important couple, for sure, because the guy with the gray-blue hair announced: "Our friends Tounette and Jackie Roland-Michel." Three or four members of the jury (among them the brunette and Daniel Hendrickx) applauded. As for Fouquières, he didn't even deign to honor them with a glance. They inclined their heads in a synchronized bow. They looked quite fit, the two of them, and most pleased with themselves.

"Number 32. Mademoiselle Yvonne Jacquet and Doctor René Meinthe." I thought I was going to faint. At first I couldn't see anything, as if I'd suddenly jumped up after spending the whole day lying on a sofa. And the voice that pronounced their names reverberated on all sides. I gripped the shoulder of someone sitting in front of me and realized too late that it was André de Fouquières. He turned around. I stammered some feeble excuses. It was impossible for me to remove my hand from his shoulder. I had to lean back and bring my arm to my chest, little by little, tensing my body to combat the heavy torpor I felt. I didn't see them drive up in the Dodge. Meinthe stopped the car in front of the jury. The headlights were on. My faintness gave way to a sort of euphoria, in which my perceptions became abnormally sharp. Meinthe sounded the horn three times, and several judges looked somewhat astonished. Fouquières himself seemed interested. Daniel Hendrickx had a smile on his face, but in my opinion it was forced. Besides, was it really a smile? No, a frozen sneer. They didn't budge from the car. Meinthe was flashing the headlights on and off. What did he think he was doing? He turned on the windshield wipers. Yvonne's face was smooth, impenetrable. And suddenly, Meinthe jumped. A murmur ran through the jury, the spectators. There was no comparison between this jump and the one he'd made at Friday's "rehearsal." Not content with clearing the door, he bounded up over it, rose into the air, spread his legs crisply, and made a nimble landing, all in one fluid movement, a single electrical discharge. And I could sense so much rage, nervousness, and fanciful provocation in his gesture that I applauded. He walked around the Dodge, stopping from time to time and standing stock-still, as though he were crossing a minefield. Every member of the jury was watching him, openmouthed. He seemed to be in certain danger, and when he finally opened the door, some judges breathed a sigh of relief.

She got out in her white dress. The dog followed her languidly. But she didn't march up and down in front of the jury as the other contestants had done. She leaned on the hood of the car and stood there gazing at Fouquières, Hendrickx, and the others while an insolent smile curled her lips. Then, with an unforeseeable gesture, she pulled off her turban and tossed it nonchalantly behind her. She ran a hand through her hair to spread it out over her shoulders. The dog jumped up on one of the Dodge's fenders and immediately assumed his sphinx position. She caressed him with a distracted hand. Behind her, Meinthe sat at the steering wheel and waited.

When I think about her today, that's the image that comes back to me most often. Her smile and her red hair. The black-and-white dog beside her. The beige Dodge. And Meinthe, barely visible behind the windshield. And the switched-on headlights. And the rays of the sun.

She slowly slid toward the door and opened it without taking her eyes off the jury. Then she got back into the car. The dog leaped onto the rear seat so casually that when I evoke the scene in detail, I seem to see him jumping in slow motion. And the Dodge — but maybe one shouldn't trust one's memories — exits the rotary in reverse. And Meinthe (this gesture is also in slow motion) tosses a rose. It lands on Daniel Hendrickx's jacket. He picks up the rose and stares at it dumbfounded. He doesn't know what to do with it. He doesn't even dare place it on the table. At last he breaks into a stupid laugh and hands the rose to his neighbor, the brunette whose name I don't know but who must be the school board president's wife, or the Chavoires golf club president's wife. Or, who knows? Madame Sandoz.

Before the car reenters the drive, Yvonne turns and waves to the jury. I even think she blows them all a kiss.

They deliberate in undertones. Three of the Sporting Club's swimming instructors have asked us politely to move a few meters away so as not to violate the privacy of the discussion. Every judge has a sheet of paper with the names and numbers of the various contestants. As each couple passed, they were supposed to be given a grade.

The judges scribble something on bits of paper and fold them. Then they put the ballots in a pile and Hendrickx shuffles and reshuffles them with his tiny manicured hands, which contrast so strongly with his build and his thickness. He's also in charge of counting the ballots. He announces names and numbers — Hatmer, 14; Tissot, 16; Roland-Michel, 17; Azuelos, 12 — but it's no use straining my ears, I can't make out most of the names. The man with the wavy coiffure and the gourmand's lips writes the numbers in a notebook. Then there's another animated confabulation. The most vehement talkers are Hendrickx, the brunette, and the man with the gray-blue hair. This last-named individual smiles incessantly, in order — I suppose — to display two rows of superb teeth, and he imagines he's charming the company by looking around and batting his eyes and trying to appear ingenuous and surprised at everything. Pouty, impatient mouth. A gastronome, without a doubt. And also what's called in slang a "lech." There must be an ongoing rivalry between him and Doudou Hendrickx. They compete for women, I'd lay money on it. But for the moment, they affect a solemn, responsible air, like company directors at a board meeting.

Fouquières, for his part, is completely uninterested in it all. He scribbles on his sheet of paper, his knitted brow expressing ironic disdain. What does he see? What scene from his past is he dreaming about? His last meeting with Lucie Delarue-Mardrus? Hendrickx leans toward him, very respectfully, and asks him a question. Fouquières replies without even looking at him. Hendrickx next goes over to query Ganonge (or Gamange), the "filmmaker," who's sitting at a table in the back on the right. Then he goes back to the man with the gray-blue hair. They have a brief altercation, and I hear them say the name "Roland-Michel" several times. Finally, "Grayblue Waves"—that's what I'll call him—steps up to a microphone and announces in an icy voice: "Ladies and gentlemen, in one minute, we are going to give you the results of this year's Houligant Elegance Cup."

I feel faint again. Everything gets blurry around me. I wonder where Yvonne and Meinthe can be. Are they waiting in the place where I left them, alongside the tennis court? What if they've abandoned me?

"By five votes to four"—Grayblue Waves's voice gets higher and higher—"I repeat: by five votes to four cast for our friends the Roland-Michels" (he stresses *our friends*, hitting the syllables hard, and now his voice is as high-pitched as a woman's), "who are well known and appreciated by all, and whose good sportsmanship I cannot commend enough…and who deserved—in my personal opinion—to win this Elegance Cup…" (he bangs his fist on the table, but his voice breaks more and more) ". . . the Cup has been awarded" (he marks a pause) "to Mademoiselle Yvonne Jacquet, escorted by Monsieur René Meinthe."

I admit it, I had tears in my eyes.

They had to make one last appearance before the jury to receive the Cup. All the children left the beach, joined the other spectators, and waited with great excitement. The musicians of the Sporting Club orchestra had taken up their usual position, under the big green-and-white striped canopy in the middle of the terrace. They were tuning their instruments.

The Dodge appeared. Yvonne was half reclining on the hood. Meinthe drove slowly. She jumped to the ground and walked very timidly toward the jury. There was a great deal of applause.

Hendrickx came down to her, brandishing the Cup. He gave it to her and kissed both her cheeks. And then other people gathered to congratulate her. André de Fouquières himself shook her hand, and she had no idea who the old gentleman was. Meinthe rejoined her. He glanced around the terrace of the Sporting Club and spotted me at once. He called out, "Victor...Victor..." and waved vigorously. I ran to him. I was saved. I would have liked to kiss Yvonne, but she was already quite surrounded. Some waiters, each carrying two trays of glasses filled with champagne, tried to make their way through the press. The whole crowd was toasting, drinking, chattering in the sun. Meinthe remained at my side, mute and impenetrable behind his dark glasses. A few meters away, a very agitated Hendrickx was introducing the brunette, Gamonge (or Ganonge), and two or three other people to Yvonne. She was thinking about something else. About me? I didn't dare believe that.

Everybody was having more and more fun. They were laughing, calling out, pressing against one another. The orchestra leader asked Meinthe and me to tell him what "piece" he ought to perform in honor of the Cup and "its lovely winner." We were stumped for a minute, but since

PATRICK MODIANO

my name was provisionally Chmara and I felt I had a gypsy heart, I asked him to play "Dark Eyes."

A "soirée" had been arranged at the Sainte-Rose to celebrate this fifth Houligant Cup and Yvonne, the conquering heroine. For the occasion, she'd selected a lamé dress the color of old gold.

She'd put the Cup on the night table, next to the Maurois book. The Cup was, in reality, a statuette of a dancer *en pointe* on a little pedestal engraved in Gothic letters: HOULIGANT CUP. 1ST PRIZE, with the year inscribed below.

Before we left, she caressed it with her hand and then flung her arms around my neck. "Don't you think it's marvelous?" she asked.

She wanted me to wear my monocle and I agreed to do so, because this was an evening unlike any other.

Meinthe had on a pale green suit, very soft, very new. Throughout the trip to Voirens, he made fun of the members of the jury. "Grayblue Waves's" real name was Raoul Fossorié, and he was the head of the tourist information office. The brunette was married to the president of the Chavoires golf club, and yes, on occasion she flirted with that "big ox" Doudou Hendrickx. Meinthe loathed him. He was a character, Meinthe told me, who'd been doing his playboy-of-the-ski-slopes number for the past thirty years. (I thought about the hero of *Liebesbriefe auf der Berg*, Yvonne's movie.) Hendrickx had ruled the night at L'Équipe and the Chamois in Megève in 1943, but now he was past fifty and looked more and more like "a satyr." Again and again Meinthe punctuated his tirade by asking, in a tone heavy with irony and innuendo, "Isn't that right, Yvonne? Isn't that right, Yvonne?" Why? And how was it that he and Yvonne were so familiar with all those people?

When we stepped out onto the pergola terrace at the Sainte-Rose, Yvonne was greeted with a little halfhearted applause. It came from a table of about ten people, with Hendrickx presiding. He made a sign to us. A photographer stood up and blinded us with his flash. The manager, the man called Pulli, pushed up three chairs for us and then came back with an orchid, which he offered with great enthusiasm to Yvonne. She thanked him.

"On this great day, the honor is all mine, Mademoiselle. And brava!"

He had an Italian accent. He made a bow to Meinthe.

"Monsieur…?" he said to me, doubtless embarrassed at not knowing me by name.

"Victor Chmara."

"Ah…Chmara?" He looked surprised and furrowed his brow.

"Monsieur Chmara…"

"Yes."

He gave me an odd look.

"I'll be with you right away, Monsieur Chmara…"

And he headed for the stairs that led to the bar on the ground floor.

Yvonne was sitting next to Hendrickx, and Meinthe and I found ourselves opposite them. Among my neighbors, I recognized the brunette from the jury, Tounette and Jackie Roland-Michel, and a man with very short gray hair and the energetic features of a former aviator or soldier: the golf club president, surely. Raoul Fossorié was at the end of the table, chewing on a match. As for the three or four other people sitting with us, including two very suntanned blondes, I was seeing them for the first time.

There wasn't a big crowd at the Sainte-Rose that evening. It was still early. The orchestra was playing a song much in the air back then, "L'amour, c'est comme un jour," while one of the musicians whispered the words:

Love, it's like a day
It goes away, it goes away
Love

Hendrickx had his right arm around Yvonne's shoulders, and I wondered what he thought he was doing. I turned to Meinthe. He was hiding behind another pair of sunglasses, this one with massive tortoiseshell earpieces, and drumming nervously on the edge of the table. I didn't dare speak to him.

"So you're happy to have your Cup?" Hendrickx asked in a wheedling voice.

Yvonne shot me an embarrassed look.

"I had a little something to do with it…"

But sure, he must be a decent guy. Why was I always so distrustful of everyone?

"Fossorié was against it. Right, Raoul? You were against it…"

And Hendrickx burst out laughing. Fossorié inhaled a lungful of cigarette smoke. He was affecting a great calm. "Not at all, Daniel, not at all," he said. "You're wrong…"

And he molded the syllables in a way I found obscene. "Hypocrite!" Hendrickx exclaimed, without any malice at all.

This reply made the brunette laugh, along with the two tanned blondes (one of their names suddenly comes back to me: Meg Devillers) and even the fellow who looked like an ex–cavalry officer. The Roland-Michels made an effort to join in the general mirth, but their hearts weren't in it. Yvonne winked at me. Meinthe kept drumming on the table.

"Your favorites," Hendrickx went on, "were Jackie and Tounette, weren't they, Raoul?" Then, turning to Yvonne: "You should shake hands with our friends the Roland-Michels, your unsuccessful rivals…"

Yvonne did so. Jackie put on a jovial expression, but Tounette Roland-Michel looked Yvonne straight in the eye. She seemed angry at her.

"One of your admirers?" asked Hendrickx. He was pointing to me.

"My fiancé," Yvonne boldly replied.

Meinthe raised his head. The muscles of his left cheek and the corners of his mouth twitched. His tics were back. "We forgot to introduce our friend to you," he said in a precious voice. "Count Victor Chmara."

He stressed the word *Count* and marked a pause after saying it. Then, turning to me: "You have before you one of France's all-time ski champions: Daniel Hendrickx."

Hendrickx smiled, but I could tell he didn't trust Meinthe's unpredictable reactions from one minute to the next. He'd certainly known him for a good long time.

"Of course, my dear Victor, you're much too young for that name to mean anything to you," Meinthe added.

The others waited. Hendrickx got ready to absorb the coming blow with feigned indifference.

"I don't suppose you were born when Daniel Hendrickx won the combined…"

"René, why do you say things like that?" Fossorié asked in a very mild, very unctuous tone, molding his syllables even more thoroughly, working his mouth so much you expected cotton candy to come out of it.

"*I* was there when he won the grand slalom and the combined," declared one of the bronzed blondes, the one named Meg Devillers. "It wasn't so long ago."

Hendrickx shrugged, and as the orchestra was starting to play a slow fox-trot, he seized the moment and asked Yvonne to dance. Fossorié, escorting Meg Devillers, joined them. The golf club president led out the other bronzed blonde. And the Roland-Michels, holding hands, followed them onto the dance floor. Meinthe bowed to the brunette and said, "Well, shall we dance a little too?"

I remained alone at the table. I didn't take my eyes off of Yvonne and Hendrickx. From a distance, he had rather an imposing presence: he was about five feet eleven inches tall, maybe even a bit over six feet. And the light shining on the dance floor — blue with a hint of pink — softened his face, canceling its thickness and its vulgarity. He was holding Yvonne very close. What should I do? Break his jaw? My hands were trembling. I could, of course, take him by surprise and punch him right in the nose. Or I could come up behind him and smash a bottle on his skull. And what good would that do? In the first place, it would make me look ridiculous in front of Yvonne. And besides, that sort of behavior wasn't suited to my mild temperament or my natural pessimism or a certain cowardice I couldn't deny.

The orchestra segued to another slow tune, and none of the couples left the dance floor. Hendrickx held Yvonne closer and closer. Why was she letting him do that? I was hoping she'd wink at me on the sly, give me a smile of complicity. No such luck. Pulli, the fat, velvet-eyed manager, cautiously approached my table. He stood right beside me, leaning on the back of one of the empty chairs. He was trying to converse with me. I felt bored by the prospect.

"Monsieur Chmara...Monsieur Chmara..."

Out of politeness, I turned to him.

"Tell me, are you related to the Chmaras of Alexandria?"

He leaned toward me avidly, and I realized why I'd chosen that name, which I thought had sprung from my imagination: it belonged to a family in Alexandria my father had often talked to me about.

"Yes. They're relatives of mine," I replied.

"So you're originally from Egypt?"

"More or less."

He smiled as though touched. He wanted to know more, and I could have talked to him about the villa in Sidi Bishr where I spent a few years of my childhood, or about the Abdeen Palace and the Auberge des Pyramides, which I very vaguely remember. And I in my turn could have asked him if he himself was related to one of my father's shady connections, a certain Antonio Pulli, who served as King Farouk's confidant and "secretary." But I was too preoccupied by Yvonne and Hendrickx.

She was still dancing with the guy, who was not only over the hill but who also certainly dyed his hair. But maybe she was doing that for some special reason she'd divulge to me later, when we were alone. Or maybe for no reason at all, just like that? What if she'd forgotten me? I've never had a great deal of confidence in my identity, and the thought that she might not recognize me again crossed my mind. Pulli sat down in Meinthe's place.

"I knew Henri Chmara in Cairo…We used to meet every evening at the Chez Groppi or the Mena House."

You would have thought he was telling me state secrets.

"Wait…It was the year when the king was going around with that French chanteuse…You know the one I mean?"

"Oh, yes…"

He spoke more and more softly. He was afraid of invisible policemen. "And you? You lived there?"

Only a weak pink glow now came from the spotlights trained on the dance floor. I lost sight of Yvonne and Hendrickx for an instant, but they reappeared behind Meinthe, Meg Devillers, Fossorié, and Tounette Roland-Michel. Tounette made a remark over her husband's shoulder. Yvonne burst out laughing.

"You understand how it is, you can't forget Egypt… No…There are evenings when I ask myself what I'm doing here…"

At once I asked myself the same question. Why hadn't I stayed where I was, at the Lindens, reading my phone directories and my movie magazines? He put his hand on my shoulder and said, "I don't know what I'd give to be sitting on the terrace at the Pastroudis…How can you ever forget Egypt?"

"But it can't be the same anymore," I murmured.

"Do you really think so?"

Out on the floor, Hendrickx was taking advantage of the semidarkness to run a hand over her behind.

Meinthe came back to our table. Alone. The brunette was dancing with another partner. He dropped into his chair.

"What were you talking about?" He'd taken off his sunglasses and was looking at me with a kindly smile. "I'm sure Pulli was telling you some of his Egyptian stories…"

"This gentleman is from Alexandria, like me," Pulli said sharply.

"You are, Victor?"

Hendrickx was trying to kiss her neck, but she held him off and jerked away from him.

"Pulli's been running this club for ten years," Meinthe was saying. "He works in Geneva in the winter. The thing is, he's never been able to get used to the mountains."

He'd noticed that I was watching Yvonne dance, and he was trying to distract my attention.

"If you come to Geneva in the winter, Victor," Meinthe said, "I'll have to take you to his place. Pulli has exactly recreated a Cairo restaurant that's not there anymore. What was its name?"

"The Khédival."

"When he's there, he imagines he's still in Egypt, and then he doesn't feel quite so blue. Isn't that right, Pulli?"

"Fuck mountains!"

"You mustn't ever feel blue," Meinthe sang softly. "Never blue. Never blue. Never."

The dancers were beginning another dance. Meinthe leaned toward me and said, "Don't pay any attention, Victor."

The Roland-Michels came back to the table. Then Fossorié and the blond Meg Devillers. And finally, Yvonne and Hendrickx. She sat down beside me and took hold of my hand. So she hadn't forgotten me. Hendrickx was gazing at me with curiosity in his eyes.

"You're Yvonne's fiancé, then?"

"Yes indeed," Meinthe said, not giving me time to answer. "And if everything goes well, her name will soon be Countess Yvonne Chmara. How do you like that?"

He meant to provoke him, but Hendrickx kept the smile on his face.

"That sounds better than Yvonne Hendrickx, don't you think?" Meinthe added.

"And what does this young man do in life?" Hendrickx asked pompously.

"Nothing," said I, screwing my monocle into my left eye. "NOTHING, NOTHING."

"No doubt you thought our young man was a ski instructor or a shopkeeper, like you," Meinthe went on.

"Shut up or I'll break you into little pieces," Hendrickx said, and you couldn't tell whether it was a threat or a joke.

Yvonne was scratching the palm of my hand with her index fingernail. Her mind was on something else. What? The simultaneous arrival of the brunette, her energetic-looking husband, and the other blonde did nothing to lighten the atmosphere. Everyone was casting sideways glances in Meinthe's direction. What was he going to do? Insult Hendrickx? Throw an ashtray at his head? Cause a scandal? In the end, the president of the golf club tried some social conversation: "Do you still have your practice in Geneva, Doctor?"

Meinthe answered him like an earnest young schoolboy: "Of course, Monsieur Tessier."

"It's amazing, how much you remind me of your father…"

Meinthe smiled sadly. "Oh, no, don't say that…my father was much better than I am."

Yvonne leaned her shoulder against mine, and that simple contact overwhelmed me. Who was *her* father? Although Hendrickx evidently liked her (or rather held her too close when they danced), I noticed that Tessier, his wife, and Fossorié hardly paid her any attention at all. Neither did the Roland-Michels. I'd even caught an expression of amused contempt on Tounette Roland-Michel's face after Yvonne shook her hand. Yvonne didn't belong to the same world they did. On the other hand, they seemed to consider Meinthe their equal and treat him with a certain indulgence. And what about me? Wasn't I a "teenager" in their eyes, a devotee of rock and roll? Perhaps not. My gravity, my monocle, and my noble title intrigued them a little. Especially Hendrickx.

"You were a skiing champion?" I asked him.

"Yes," Meinthe answered, "but that's all lost in the mists of time."

"Just imagine," Hendrickx said to me, laying his hand on my forearm, "I met this whippersnapper" — he gestured toward Meinthe — "when he was five years old. He was playing with dolls."

Fortunately, the orchestra launched into a cha-cha-cha at that moment. It was past midnight, and customers were arriving in clusters. They were bumping into one another on the dance floor. Hendrickx hailed Pulli.

"Bring us some champagne and tell the orchestra…"

He winked at Pulli, who responded with a vaguely military salute, forefinger above eyebrow.

"Doctor, do you think aspirin is good for circulation problems?" asked the president of the golf club. "I read some such thing in *Science and Life*."

Meinthe hadn't heard him. Yvonne laid her head on my shoulder. The orchestra stopped playing. Pulli brought a tray with glasses and two bottles of champagne. Hendrickx stood up and waved his arms. The couples on the dance floor, as well as the other guests, turned toward our table.

"Ladies and gentlemen," Hendrickx proclaimed, "we are going to drink to the health of the triumphant winner of the Houligant Cup, Mademoiselle Yvonne Jacquet."

He motioned to Yvonne to stand up. We all got to our feet. We clinked glasses, and as I could feel everyone's eyes on us, I faked a coughing fit.

"And now, ladies and gentlemen," Hendrickx resumed, speaking emphatically, "I ask you for a round of applause for the young and lovely Yvonne Jacquet."

People shouted "bravas" all around us. She pressed against me shyly. My monocle had fallen out. The clapping continued at length, and I didn't dare budge an inch. I fixed my eyes in front of me, on Fossorié's massive hair, on its cunning, multiple, intertwined undulations, on the curious blue-gray mane that looked like a finely wrought helmet.

The orchestra came back and the music started again. A very slow cha-cha-cha, in which you could make out the melody of "April in Portugal."

Meinthe stood up. "If it's all right with you, Hendrickx," he said (using the formal *vous* for the first time), "I am going to leave you and this elegant company." He turned to Yvonne and me: "Do you want a ride back?"

I said yes docilely. Yvonne stood up too. She shook hands with Fossorié and the president of the golf club, but she didn't dare say goodbye to the Roland-Michels or the two bronzed blondes.

"And when's the wedding going to be?" Hendrickx asked, pointing a finger at us.

"As soon as we get the hell out of this shitty little French village," I said very fast.

They all gaped at me.

Why had I spoken so stupidly and crudely about a French village? I still ask myself that, and I apologize. Meinthe himself looked sorry to see me in this new light.

"Come on," Yvonne said, taking me by the arm. Hendrickx remained speechless, staring, wide-eyed.

I bumped into Pulli without meaning to.

"Are you leaving, Monsieur Chmara?" he asked, trying to restrain me and pressing my hand.

"I'll be back, I'll be back," I told him.

"Oh, please do come back. We can talk some more about all those things…"

And he made an evasive gesture. We crossed the dance floor. Meinthe was marching behind us. Now the spotlights were making it look as though big snowflakes were falling on the dancing couples. Yvonne was hauling me along, and we had trouble getting through the crowd.

Before going down the steps, I tried to take a last look at the table where we'd been sitting.

All my rage had dissolved, and I regretted my loss of self-control.

"Are you coming?" Yvonne said. "Are you coming?"

"What are you thinking, Victor?" Meinthe asked, tapping me on the shoulder.

I stayed there at the top of the stairs, hypnotized once again by Fossorié's hair. It was gleaming. He must have smeared it with some kind of phosphorescent brilliantine. How much effort, how much patience, to erect that gray-blue edifice every morning.

Back in the Dodge, Meinthe said our evening had been a stupid waste of time. Daniel Hendrickx was to blame for recommending that Yvonne should come and telling her that all the contest judges would be there, as well as several journalists. It was a mistake ever to believe "that scumbag."

"As you well know, my dear," Meinthe added in an exasperated voice. "Did he at least give you the check?"

"Of course."

And then I got the scoop about the great triumph: Hendrickx had created the Houligant Cup five years before. In alternate years it was awarded in winter, at l'Alpe d'Huez or Megève. He'd begun this undertaking out of snobbism (he chose prominent socialites as judges), as a way of getting publicity (the newspapers that reported on the Cup would quote him, Hendrickx, and cite his athletic accomplishments), and because of his hankering for pretty girls. Given the promise of winning the Cup, any idiot would yield to him. The check was for 800,000 francs. In the jury's deliberations, Hendrickx's word was law. Fossorié would have liked the Elegance Cup, which was a big hit every year, to be a bit more dependent on the tourist office. That was the reason for the muted rivalry between the two men.

"Ah, yes, my dear Victor," Meinthe concluded, "now you see how petty the provinces are."

He turned and favored me with a sad smile. We'd arrived in front of the Casino, and Yvonne asked Meinthe to drop us off there. We'd walk back to the hotel, we said.

"Call me tomorrow, you two." He seemed woebegone because we were leaving him on his own. He leaned out the window: "And forget this dreadful evening."

Then he sped off, as if he wanted to tear himself away from us. He took Rue Royale, and I wondered where he would spend the night.

We admired the changing colors of the fountain for a few minutes. We got as close to it as we could, and water droplets sprayed our faces. I shoved Yvonne. She struggled and cried out. Then she tried to take me by surprise and push me too. Our shouts of laughter echoed across the deserted esplanade. Not far away, the waiters at the Taverne were just about finished clearing the tables. The night was warm, and I felt a kind of intoxication at the thought that the summer had hardly begun and that we still had days and days ahead to spend together, and evenings when we could go out for walks or stay in the room and listen to the muffled, idiotic plunking of the tennis balls.

On the first floor of the Casino, the bay windows were all lit up: the baccarat room. You could see silhouettes. We walked around the building, which had CASINO inscribed in round letters on its façade, and we passed the entrance to the Brummel Lounge, where the music we heard was coming from. Yes, that was a summer of music, there were tunes and songs in the air, always the same ones.

We walked along Avenue d'Albigny on the left-hand sidewalk, which bordered the garden of the prefecture. Not many cars passed us, only a few in either direction. I asked Yvonne why she let Hendrickx put his hand on her behind. She answered that it didn't mean anything. She had to be nice to Hendrickx, because he'd let her win the Cup, and he'd given her a check for 800,000 francs. I told her that in my opinion, a girl should ask for a lot more than 800,000 francs to let someone "grope her butt," and that in any case the Houligant Elegance Cup was of no interest to anyone. Not to anyone at all. Except for a few stray provincials scattered on the shores of a godforsaken lake, nobody knew that Cup existed. It was grotesque, the Houligant Cup. And pathetic. Wasn't it? In the first place, what did anybody in this "Savoyard backwater" know about elegance? What? She answered in a pinched little voice, saying she found Hendrickx "very attractive" and was thrilled to have danced with him. I said—making an effort to articulate the syllables, but it was no use, I swallowed half of them anyway—that Hendrickx had a bull's head and "a saggy ass, like all the French." "But you're French too," she said. "No. No. I've got nothing to do with the French," I said. "You French, you're incapable of understanding true nobility, true—" She burst out laughing; I didn't intimidate her. So, faking extreme coldness, I declared that in the future she'd be best advised not to boast too much about the Houligant Elegance Cup, if she didn't want people making fun of her. There were lots of girls who had won ridiculous little prizes like that shortly before sinking into utter oblivion. And how many others had accidentally got a part in a worthless film like *Liebesbriefe auf der Berg*? Their cinematic career had come to an end right there. Many were called. Few were chosen. "You think the movie's worthless?" she asked. "Totally." That one made her suffer, I think. She walked on without saying anything. We sat on the bench in the chalet and waited for the cable car. With meticulous care, she tore an old cigarette pack into tiny shreds. As she proceeded, she placed the little pieces of paper on the ground, and they were like a pile of confetti. Her concentration moved me so much that I kissed her hands.

The cable car stopped before it got to Saint-Charles-Carabacel. Some sort of breakdown, obviously, but nobody would be coming to fix it at that hour of the night. She was even more passionate than usual. I thought she must love me a little after all. Now and then we looked out the window and found ourselves suspended between heaven and earth, with the lake down below, and the roofs. Dawn was coming on.

The next day there was a long article on page three of *L'Écho-Liberté*, under the headline, "Houligant Elegance Cup Awarded for the Fifth Time":

Late yesterday morning at the Sporting Club, a large crowd watched with interest the proceedings of the fifth Houligant Elegance Cup. The organizers, having awarded the cup last year at Megève during the winter, chose to make this year's contest a summer event. The sun kept its appointment. Never has it shone so gloriously. Most of the spectators were in beach attire. Among them we noticed M. Jean Marchat of the Comédie-Française, here to star in several performances of *Listen Up, Gentlemen* at the Casino theater.

As usual, the jury brought together a wide variety of well-known personalities. It was presided over by M. André de Fouquières, who was kind enough to grant this Cup the benefit of his long experience; indeed, we might well say that M. de Fouquières, in Paris as in Deauville, in Cannes or Le Touquet, has been both the epitome and the arbiter of the elegant life for the past fifty years.

Seated around him were: Daniel Hendrickx, the well-known ski champion and the promoter of this Cup; Fossorié, of the tourist information office; Gamange, the film director; M. and Mme. Tessier of the golf club; M. and Mme. Sandoz of the Windsor; the sub-prefect, M. P. A. Roquevillard. The absence of the dancer José Torres, detained at the last minute, was regretted.

The great majority of the contestants did honor to the contest; M. and Mme. Jacques Roland-Michel of Lyon, who are sojourning, as they do every summer, in their villa in Chavoires, drew particular attention and were vigorously applauded.

But the prize, after several ballots, was awarded to Mlle. Yvonne Jacquet, 22, a lovely young woman with red hair, dressed in white and accompanied by a formidable mastiff. Mlle. Jacquet's grace and nonconformism made a vivid impression on the jury.

Mlle. Yvonne Jacquet was born and raised in our town. Her family is originally from the region. She has just made her cinematic debut in a film shot a few kilometers from here by a German filmmaker. We wish Mlle. Jacquet, our hometown girl, good luck and much success.

Her escort was M. René Meinthe, the son of Dr. Henri Meinthe. This name will awaken many memories in some of our readers. Indeed, Dr. Henri Meinthe, the scion of an old Savoyard family, was one of the heroes and martyrs of the Resistance. A street in our town bears his name.

The article was illustrated by a large photograph taken at the Sainte-Rose, just at the moment when we entered. It shows all three of us on our feet, Yvonne and me side by side in the foreground, Meinthe a little behind. The caption below the photo reads, "Mlle. Yvonne Jacquet, M. René Meinthe, and one of their friends, Count Victor Chmara." The picture's very sharp, in spite of the newsprint. Yvonne and I look serious. Meinthe's smiling. We're all gazing at a point in the middle distance. I carried that photograph on me for many years before putting it away with other souvenirs, and one night when I was looking at it and feeling gloomy, I couldn't stop myself from writing across it in red pencil: "Royals for a day."

8.

"The lightest port you've got, my dear," Meinthe says again.

The barmaid doesn't understand. "Light?"

"Very, very light." But he says it without conviction.

He runs his hand over his unshaven cheeks. Twelve years ago, he would shave two or three times a day. Somewhere in the depths of the Dodge's glove compartment, there was an electric razor, but he called it a useless instrument, because his beard was too stiff. He even broke some Bleue Extra blades on it.

The barmaid comes back with a bottle of Sandeman and pours him a glass. "I don't have any...light port," she says.

She whispers "light" as though it's a dirty word.

"Doesn't matter, my dear," Meinthe replies.

And he smiles. All at once he seems younger. He breathes into his glass and observes the ripples on the surface of the port.

"Would you by chance have a straw, my dear?"

She brings him one reluctantly, her face a sullen mask. She's not more than twenty. She must be saying to herself, "How long is this moron going to stay here? And how about the other one over there, the loon in the checked jacket?" As she does every night at eleven, she has just relieved Geneviève, who was already working in this bar in the early '60s and who also, during the day, ran the refreshment stall near the bathing huts at the Sporting Club. A gracious blonde. It was said she had a heart murmur.

Meinthe is turned toward the man in the checked jacket. That jacket's the only noticeable thing about him. Otherwise, he's got a thoroughly ordinary face: small black mustache, rather large nose, brown hair combed back. A moment ago he looked decidedly drunk, but now he's sitting up very straight, with a self-important smirk on his lips.

"Will you call…" (his voice is thick and hesitant) "Chambéry 233 for me…"

The barmaid dials the number. Somebody answers on the other end. But the man in the checked jacket remains at his table, stiff and straight.

"Monsieur, I have your party on the line," the barmaid says, getting anxious.

He doesn't budge an inch. His eyes are wide open and his chin thrust slightly forward.

"Monsieur…"

He's a stone statue. She hangs up. She must be starting to worry. These two customers are really bizarre…Meinthe has been observing the goings-on with a frown. After a few minutes, the other man starts up again, his voice even more muted than before:

"Will you call…Chambéry 233 for me…"

The barmaid doesn't move. He goes on imperturbably: "Will you call…"

She shrugs. Then Meinthe leans over to the telephone and dials the number himself. When a voice answers, he holds out the receiver toward the man in the checked jacket, who doesn't move. He fixes his wide-open eyes on Meinthe.

"Come now, Monsieur…" Meinthe murmurs. "Come now…"

Finally he shrugs and lays the receiver on the bar.

"Perhaps you'd like to be home in bed, my dear?" he asks the barmaid. "I don't want to keep you."

"No. Anyway, we don't close until two in the morning…A lot of people will be coming in later."

"A lot?"

"There's a convention. They'll all end up here."

She pours herself a glass of Coca-Cola.

"Not very merry here in the winter, is it?" Meinthe remarks.

"I'm going to Paris," she declares aggressively.

"The right move."

The man at the table behind him snaps his fingers: "Could I have another dry martini, please?" Then he adds: "And Chambéry 233…"

Meinthe dials the number again and, without turning around, places the receiver on the stool next to him. The girl giggles. He raises his head, and his eyes fall on the old photographs of Émile Allais and James Couttet above the aperitif bottles. Another photo has been added, one of Daniel Hendrickx, who was killed in an automobile accident a few years ago. Surely Geneviève, the other barmaid, had it hung up there. She was in love with Hendrickx in the days when she worked at the Sporting Club. In the days of the Houligant Cup.

9.

That cup — where is it now? In the back of what closet? Or what storeroom? In the end, we used it for an ashtray. The pedestal the dancer was on had a convenient circular rim. We crushed out our cigarettes on it. We must have left it behind in the hotel room, and I'm surprised that I — attached to objects as I am — didn't take it with me.

At first, however, Yvonne seemed to dote on it. She displayed it prominently on the desk in the living room. It marked the start of her career. The Victoires and the Oscars would come later. Later still, she'd refer to it with affection when talking to journalists, for I had no doubt that Yvonne would become a movie star. In the meanwhile, we pinned up the long article from *L'Écho-Liberté*.

We spent lazy days. We'd get up fairly early. In the morning, there was often mist — or rather a blue vapor that freed us from the law of gravity. We were light, so light...When we went down Boulevard Carabacel, we hardly touched the sidewalk. Nine o'clock. Soon the thin mist would be burned away by the sun. No guests yet on the beach at the Sporting Club. We were the only living creatures, except for one of the beach attendants, dressed in white, who was putting out deck chairs and parasols.

Yvonne wore an opal-colored two-piece bathing suit, and I'd borrow her beach robe. She'd go swimming, and I'd watch her. The dog too would follow her with his eyes. She'd wave and shout to me, laughing, to come in and join her. I used to tell myself it was all too good to be true, and that some disaster was going to happen tomorrow. On July 12, 1939, I'd think, a guy like me, wearing a red-and-green striped beach robe, was watching his fiancée swim in the pool at the Éden-Roc. He was afraid, like me, to listen to the radio. Even there, at Cap d'Antibes, he wouldn't escape the war...The names of possible places of refuge jostled one another in his head, but he wouldn't have time to desert. For a few seconds, I was seized by an inexplicable terror, and then she got out of the water and came and lay down beside me in the sun.

Around eleven o'clock, when the beach at the Sporting Club started to be overrun by people, we'd take refuge in a kind of small cove. You could reach it from the restaurant terrace by going down some crumbling steps built in Gordon-Gramme's time. Below, a beach of shingles and rocks, and a tiny one-room cabin with windows and shutters. On the rickety door, carved into the wood in Gothic letters, two initials: G-G — Gordon-Gramme — and the date: 1903. He must surely have built that doll's house himself and come there to gather his thoughts. Sensitive, farsighted Gordon-Gramme. When the sun was beating down too hard, we'd spend a little while inside. Semidarkness. A pool of light on the threshold. A slight odor of mold, which we eventually got used to. The sound of the lapping water, as monotonous and reassuring as the tennis balls. We'd shut the door.

She swam and sunbathed. I preferred the shade, like my Eastern ancestors. In the early afternoon, we'd go back up to the Hermitage and stay in our room until seven or eight o'clock in the evening. There was a very wide balcony, and Yvonne would stretch out in the middle of it. I'd install myself at her side, my head covered by a white felt "colonial" hat — one of the few things I still owned that had belonged to my father, and all the more precious because we were together when he bought it. It was at Sport et Climat, on the corner of Boulevard Saint-Germain and Rue Saint-Dominique. I was eight years old, and my father was getting ready to leave for Brazzaville. What was he going to do there? He never told me.

I went down to the lobby to get magazines. Because of the foreign clientele, you could find most of the major European publications there. I'd buy them all: *Oggi*, *Life*, *Cinémonde*, *Der Stern*, *Confidential*…I'd cast a wary glance at the big newspaper headlines. There were some serious goings-on in Algeria, but also in France and elsewhere in the world. I preferred not to know. A lump formed in my throat. I hoped there wouldn't be too much talk about all that in the illustrated magazines. No. No. Avoid important topics. Panic would take hold of me again. To calm myself, I'd down an Alexandra at the bar and go back upstairs with my pile of magazines. We'd read them, sprawled on the bed or the floor in front of the open French window, amid the golden patches strewn by the last rays of the sun. Lana Turner's daughter had stabbed her mother's lover to death. Errol Flynn had died of a heart attack, but not before responding to a young friend who asked him where she could put the ashes of her cigarette by gesturing at the open mouth of a stuffed leopard. Henri Garat had died like a tramp. Prince Ali Khan had died too, in a car crash near Suresnes. I can't remember any of the happy events. We'd clip out a few photos. We hung them on the walls of the room, and the hotel management didn't seem to mind.

Empty afternoons. Slow hours. Yvonne often wore a black silk dressing gown with red dots and some holes here and there. I'd forget to take off my old "colonial" fedora.

The partly torn-up magazines littered the floor. Bottles of suntan lotion were everywhere. The dog lay across an armchair. And we listened to records on the old Teppaz player. We'd forget to turn on the lights.

Downstairs the orchestra would be starting to play and people began arriving for dinner. Between two numbers, we'd hear the babble of conversations. A voice would rise above the hubbub — a woman's voice — or a burst of laughter. And the orchestra would start up again. I'd leave the French window open so that the commotion and the music could reach up to us. They were our protection. And they began at the same time every day, hence the world was still going around. For how long?

The open bathroom door framed a rectangle of light. Yvonne was putting on her makeup. I'd lean over the balcony and watch all those people (most of them in evening attire), the shuttling waiters, and the musicians, whose individual characteristics I came to know by heart. For example, the orchestra leader stood leaning forward, his chin practically against his chest. And when the piece came to an end, he'd jerk his head upward, openmouthed, like a man gasping for breath. The violinist had a nice, rather piggy face; he closed his eyes and nodded, sniffing the air.

Yvonne was ready. I'd turn on a lamp. She'd smile at me and give me a mysterious look. By way of amusing herself, she'd put on black gloves that went up to her elbows. She'd stand in the middle of the room, surrounded by disorder, the unmade bed, the scattered articles of clothing. We'd leave on tiptoe, avoiding the dog, the ashtrays, the record player, and the empty glasses.

Late into the night, after Meinthe had brought us back to the hotel, we'd listen to music. Our nearest neighbors lodged several complaints about the "racket" we made. They were — as the concierge informed me — an industrialist from Lyon and his wife, whom I'd seen shaking hands with Fossorié after the Houligant Cup. I had a bouquet of peonies brought to them, with a note: "Count Chmara apologizes and sends you these flowers."

Upon our return, the dog would bark, plaintively and regularly, and that would go on for about an hour. It was impossible to calm him. So we'd opt for putting on music to drown out his barking. While Yvonne undressed and took a bath, I'd read her some pages from the Maurois book. We'd leave the record player on, blasting out some frenetic song. I would vaguely hear the industrialist from Lyon pounding

on the door between our rooms and the telephone ring-
ing. He must have complained to the night porter. Maybe
they'd wind up kicking us out of the hotel. So much the
better. Yvonne had slipped on her beach robe, and we
were preparing a meal for the dog (we had for this purpose
a whole pile of cans and even a portable stove). After he
ate, we hoped, he'd shut up. The Lyon industrialist's wife
shouted through the din the singer was making: "Do something, Henri, *do* something. CALL THE POLICE..." Their
balcony adjoined ours. We'd left the French window open,
and the industrialist, weary of beating on the communicat-
ing door, started reviling us from outside. So Yvonne took
off her robe and stepped out onto the balcony, completely
naked, except that she'd pulled on her long black gloves.
The man stared at her and went red in the face. His wife
was pulling him by the arm. And bawling: "Oh, the filthy
bastards...The whore..."

We were young.

And rich. The drawer of her night table was overflowing
with banknotes. Where did all that money come from? I
didn't dare ask her. But one day, while arranging the wads
in neat rows so she could close the drawer, she explained
that it was her earnings from the film. She'd insisted on
being paid in cash, in 5,000-franc notes. She added that
she'd also cashed the Houligant Cup check. She showed
me a package wrapped in newspaper: eight hundred 1,000-
franc banknotes. She preferred the smaller denominations.

She kindly offered to lend me some money, but I
declined. There were still 800,000 or 900,000 francs lying

around in my suitcases. I'd acquired that sum by selling a bookseller in Geneva two "rare" editions I'd bought for a song in a Paris junk shop. At the hotel reception desk, I exchanged my 50,000-franc notes for the equivalent in bills of 500 francs, which I carried upstairs in a beach bag. I emptied them all out on the bed. She put all her banknotes on the bed too, and together they formed an impressive pile. We marveled at that mass of paper money, which we wouldn't be long in spending. And I recognized in her our shared taste for ready cash, I mean for money easily won, the wads you stuff in your pockets, the wild money that slips through your fingers.

After the article appeared, I started asking her questions about her childhood here in this town. She'd avoid answering, no doubt because she liked to remain mysterious, and because in the arms of "Count Chmara" she was a little ashamed of her "modest" origins. And since the truth about me would have disappointed her, I told her stories about my family's adventures. My father was still very young when he left Russia with his mother and sisters, on account of the Revolution. They'd spent some time in Constantinople, Brussels, and Berlin before settling in Paris. Like many beautiful, aristocratic White Russians, my aunts had earned their living working as mannequins at Schiaparelli. My father, at the age of twenty-five, went to America on a sailboat and there married the heiress to the Woolworth fortune. Then he divorced her and got a colossal alimony settlement. Back in France, he met my *maman*, an Irish music-hall artiste. I was born. They'd both disappeared in a light airplane over Cap Ferrat in July 1949. I'd been raised by my grandmother, in Paris, in a ground-floor apartment on Rue Lord-Byron. That was it.

Did she believe me? Halfway. Before going to sleep, she required me to tell her "fabulous" stories, full of titled people and movie stars. How many times did I describe my father's trysts with the actress Lupe Vélez in the Spanish-style villa in Beverly Hills? But when I wanted her to tell me about her family in return, she'd say, "Oh…It's not very interesting…" And yet it was the only thing I needed to make my happiness complete: the tale of a childhood and adolescence spent in a provincial town. How could I explain to her that to my eyes, the eyes of a man without a country, Hollywood, Russian princes, and Farouk's Egypt seemed drab and faded in comparison with that exotic and nearly unapproachable creature, a little French girl?

10.

It happened one evening, just like that. She told me, "We're having dinner at my uncle's." We were reading magazines on the balcony, and the cover of one of them, I remember, pictured the English actress Belinda Lee, who had died in a car accident.

I put on my flannel suit. Since the collar of my only white dress shirt was worn threadbare, I was wearing an off-white polo shirt, which went very well with my blue-and-red International Bar Fly tie. I had a lot of trouble tying the tie, because the polo shirt's collar was too soft, but I wanted to look well dressed. I accessorized my suit jacket with a midnight-blue pocket handkerchief I'd bought for its deep color. As to footwear, I hesitated among raggedy moccasins, espadrilles, and a pair of Westons, which were almost new but had thick crepe soles. I opted for the last, considering them the most dignified. Yvonne begged me to wear my monocle: it would intrigue her uncle, and he'd think I was a "hoot." But that sounded exactly like what I didn't want, and I hoped the man would see me as I really was: a modest, serious youth.

She chose a white silk dress and the fuchsia turban she'd worn on the day of the Houligant Cup. It had taken her longer than usual to put on her makeup. Her lipstick was the same color as the turban. She pulled on her elbow-length gloves, which I thought a curious thing to do before going to dinner at her uncle's. We set out, taking the dog.

Some people in the hotel lobby caught their breath as we passed. The dog preceded us, performing his quadrille figures. He'd do that when we went out at times he wasn't used to.

We took the cable car.

We proceeded along Rue du Parmelan, the continuation of Rue Royale. As we walked on, I discovered a different town. We were leaving behind us all the artificial charm of a spa resort, all that shoddy décor, fit for an operetta in which a very old Egyptian pasha falls asleep in the sorrow of exile. Food stores and motorcycle shops replaced the upscale boutiques. Yes, the number of motorcycle shops was unbelievable. Sometimes two of them adjoined each other, both with discounted Vespas out on the sidewalk. We passed the bus station. A bus was waiting, its engine running. On its side you could read the name of its company and the stops it made: SEVRIER-PRINGY-ALBERTVILLE. We reached the corner of Rue du Parmelan and Avenue du Maréchal-Leclerc. The avenue bore this name for only a short distance, because it was Route Nationale 201, which went to Chambéry. It was lined with plane trees.

The dog was afraid and kept as far away from the road as he could. The Hermitage setting better suited his weary silhouette, and his presence in the suburbs aroused curiosity. Yvonne said nothing, but the neighborhood was familiar to her. There had certainly been years and years when she'd walked that road regularly, coming back from school or from a party in town ("party" isn't the right word; she would have been to a "ball" or a "dance hall"). As for me, I'd already forgotten the lobby at the Hermitage. I didn't know where we were going, but I was already prepared to live with her on Nationale 201. The windows in our bedroom would tremble as the heavy trucks roared past, like the windows in the little apartment on Boulevard Soult where I'd lived for a few months with my father. I felt light on my feet. Except for my heels, which my new shoes were chafing a little.

Night had fallen, and on each side of the road, two- and three-story houses stood guard, little white buildings that had a kind of colonial charm. There were buildings like those in the European quarter of Tunis and even in Saigon. Every now and then, a house that looked like a mountain cabin in the middle of a minuscule garden reminded me that we were in Haute-Savoie.

We passed a brick church, and I asked Yvonne its name: Saint-Christophe. I would have loved to know if she'd made her first communion there, but I didn't dare ask the question for fear of being disappointed. A little farther on was a movie house called, in English, the Splendid. With its dirty beige façade and its red porthole doors, it looked like all the cinemas you notice in the suburbs when you cross the Avenues du Maréchal-de-Lattre-de-Tassigny, Jean-Jaurès, or du Maréchal-Leclerc, just before entering Paris. She must have gone to the Splendid too, when she was sixteen. That evening it was showing a film from our childhood, *The Prisoner of Zenda*, and I imagined us going to the box office and getting two balcony seats. I'd known that theater forever, I could see its interior, the seats with their wooden backs, the panel with local advertisements in front of the screen: Jean Chermoz, florist, 22 Rue Sommeiller. LAV NET laundry & dry cleaning, 17 Rue du Président-Favre. Decouz, Radios, TV, Hi-Fi, 23 Avenue d'Allery...We passed one café after another. Through the windows of the last one, we could see four wavy-haired boys playing table soccer. There were green tables outside. The customers sitting at them observed the dog with interest. Yvonne had taken off her long gloves. The thing was, she was returning to her natural setting, and you might have thought she'd put on her white silk dress to go to a local fête or a July 14 dance.

We walked past a dark wooden fence nearly a hundred meters long. Posters of all sorts were glued to it. Posters for the Splendid cinema. Posters announcing the parish festival and the arrival of the Pinder circus. Luis Mariano's head, half torn off. Old, barely legible slogans: FREE HENRI MARTIN...RIDGWAY GO HOME...ALGÉRIE FRANÇAISE... Arrow-pierced, initialed hearts. The streetlamps that had been installed out there were modern, concrete, slightly curved. They projected the shadows of the plane trees and their rustling foliage onto the fence. A very warm night. I removed my jacket. We were in front of the entrance to an imposing garage. To the right, a little side door bore a plaque with a name in Gothic letters: JACQUET. There was also a sign: SPARE PARTS FOR AMERICAN VEHICLES.

He was waiting for us in a ground-floor room that did double duty as a living and dining room. The two windows and the glass door overlooked the garage, which was an immense hangar.

Yvonne introduced me, noble title and all. I was embarrassed, but he seemed to find it perfectly natural. He turned to her and asked gruffly, "Does the count like breaded veal cutlets?" He had a very pronounced Parisian accent. "Because I'm making cutlets for you."

He kept a cigarette — or, rather, a butt — stuck in the corner of his mouth and screwed up his eyes as he spoke. His voice was very deep and raspy, the voice of a big drinker or heavy smoker. "Sit down…"

He pointed at a bluish sofa against the wall. Then, with little swaying steps, he walked into the next room: the kitchen. We heard frying sounds.

He came back carrying a tray, which he placed on an arm of the sofa. On the tray were three glasses and a plate of those cookies known as *langues de chat*. He handed glasses to Yvonne and me. They held a vaguely pink fluid. He smiled at me and said, "Try it. A hell of a fine cocktail. Liquid dynamite. It's called a Pink Lady…Try it."

I wet my lips with it. I swallowed a drop. And immediately began to cough. Yvonne burst out laughing.

"You shouldn't have given him that, Unky Roland."

I was touched and surprised to hear her say "Unky Roland."

"Dynamite, am I right?" he said, his eyes sparkling, practically bulging. "You have to get used to it."

He sat in the armchair, which was covered with the same tired bluish fabric as the sofa. He stroked the dog, dozing at his feet, and sipped his cocktail.

"Everything all right?" he asked Yvonne.

"Yes."

He nodded. He didn't know what else to say. Maybe he didn't feel like talking in front of someone he was meeting for the first time. He was waiting for me to launch the conversation, but I was even more intimidated than he was, and Yvonne gave us no help at all. On the contrary: she took her gloves out of her purse and slowly pulled them on. He followed this bizarre and interminable operation out of the corner of one eye and got a little sulky around the mouth. There were some long minutes of silence.

I was watching him stealthily. His hair was brown and thick and his complexion ruddy, but his large black eyes and long eyelashes gave his heavy face a certain languid charm. He must have been a beautiful young man, of a slightly stocky beauty. His lips, by contrast, were thin, humorous, very French.

You could tell he'd dressed and groomed himself carefully to receive us. Gray tweed jacket too broad across the shoulders, dark shirt with no tie. Lavender cologne. I tried to spot a family resemblance between him and Yvonne. Without success. But I figured I'd manage it before the end of the evening. I'd place myself in front of them and examine them both at the same time. In the end, I was sure to notice a gesture or a facial expression they had in common.

"So, Uncle Roland, do you have a lot of work at the moment?"

She asked the question in a tone of voice that surprised me. It mingled childish naïveté with the kind of brusqueness a woman might use in addressing the man she lives with.

"Indeed I do...These crap American cars...All these shitty Studebakers..."

"No fun, right, Unky Roland?" This time you would have thought she was talking to a child.

"No. Especially since the engines inside those goddamn Studebakers…"

He left his sentence unfinished, as if he'd suddenly realized that technical details wouldn't interest us.

"Ah, well…And how are things with you?" he asked Yvonne. "Everything all right?"

"Yes, Unky."

She was thinking about something else. What?

"Excellent. If everything's all right, that's all right… Shall we move to the table?"

He stood up and put his hand on my shoulder.

"Hey, Yvonne, did you hear me?"

The table stood close to the French window and the windows overlooking the garage. A navy-blue-and-white checkered tablecloth. Duralex tumblers. He indicated my place: the one I'd figured would be mine. Across from them. On his plate and Yvonne's, wooden napkin rings with their names — "Roland" and "Yvonne" — carved in round letters.

With his slightly swaying gait, he headed for the kitchen, and Yvonne seized the chance to scratch the palm of my hand with her fingernail. He brought us a bowl of *salade niçoise*. Yvonne served us.

"You like it, I hope?"

Then, speaking to Yvonne and stressing each syllable: "Does-the-count-real-ly-like-it?"

I detected no malice in his words, just a very Parisian irony and geniality. Though I couldn't understand why this

"Savoyard" (I remembered a sentence in the article about Yvonne: "Her family is originally from the region") spoke with the weary accents of Belleville.

No, there was definitely no resemblance. The uncle didn't have Yvonne's delicate features or long hands or slender neck. Sitting by her side, he looked yet more massive and taurine than he had in the armchair. I would have dearly liked to know where she got her green eyes and her auburn hair, but the boundless respect I feel for French families and their secrets prevented me from asking questions. Where were Yvonne's father and mother? Were they still alive? What did they do? As I continued—discreetly—to observe Yvonne and her uncle, however, I discovered that they shared some mannerisms. For example, they had the same way of holding their knives and forks, with their index fingers a little too far forward, the same slowness in bringing the forks to their mouths, and sometimes the same way of screwing up their eyes, which gave them both little wrinkles.

"And you," he said to me, "what do you do in life?"

"He doesn't do anything, Unky."

She hadn't given me time to answer.

"It's not true, Monsieur," I stammered. "Not at all. My work is…books."

"…Books? Books?" He was looking at me with incredibly vacant eyes.

"I…I…"

Yvonne fixed her gaze on me with a cheeky little smile.

"I…I'm writing a book. There."

I was totally surprised by the peremptory tone in which I'd told that lie.

"You're writing a book…? A book…?" He frowned and leaned a little closer to me: "A…crime novel?"

He looked relieved. He was smiling.

"Yes, a crime novel," I murmured. "A crime novel."

A clock struck in the next room. A scratchy, interminable chime. Yvonne listened to it openmouthed. Her uncle looked for my reaction; he was ashamed of that intrusive, distorted music, which I couldn't quite identify. But then, when he said, "There goes that goddamned Westminster again," I recognized in the cacophony the chimes of London's Big Ben, but more melancholy and more disturbing than the real thing.

"That goddamned Westminster has gone completely crazy. It chimes twelve times every hour…It's going to make me sick, that Westminster bastard…If I get my hands on it…"

He spoke of it as if it were a personal, invisible enemy.

"Do you hear me, Yvonne?"

"But I've told you, it was Mama's…All you have to do is give it back to me and we won't talk about it anymore…"

Suddenly he was very red, and I feared he would fly into a rage.

"It's staying here, you understand me? Here…"

"Of course it is, Unky, of course it is…" She shrugged. "Keep your old clock…your stupid old Westminster…"

She turned to me and winked. But he wanted to recruit me as a witness for his side too. "You understand. It would make an emptiness in my life if I didn't hear that crappy Westminster anymore…"

"It reminds me of my childhood," Yvonne said. "It used to keep me awake…"

And I saw her in her bed, clutching a teddy bear, her eyes wide open.

We heard five more notes at irregular intervals, like a drunkard's hiccups. Then Big Ben fell silent, as if forever.

I took a deep breath and turned to the uncle: "She lived here when she was little?"

I spoke so fast he didn't understand what I'd said.

"He's asking you if I lived here when I was little. Are you getting deaf, Unky?"

"But yes, up there. Upstairs." He was pointing at the ceiling.

"I'll show you my room in a little while. If it's still the same, is it, Unky?"

"It is. I haven't changed anything."

He stood up, collected our plates and cutlery, and went to the kitchen. He came back with clean plates and fresh silverware.

"Do you prefer yours well done?" he asked me.

"However you want."

"No indeed. It's however you want, YOU, your lordship."

I blushed.

"Have you decided, then? Well done or rare?"

I couldn't utter a syllable. I moved my hand, a vague gesture to gain time. He was firmly planted in front of me, his arms crossed. He looked at me with a kind of amazement in his eyes.

"Tell me, is he always like this?"

PATRICK MODIANO

"Yes, Unky, always. He's always like this."

He served us the cutlets and green peas himself, specifying that they were "fresh garden peas, not from a can." He also poured us some wine, Mercurey, which he bought only for "important guests."

"So you think he's an 'important guest'?" Yvonne asked, pointing to me.

"But of course. It's the first time in my life I've ever dined with a count. You're Count what again?"

"Chmara," Yvonne snapped, as if she was angry with him for forgetting my name.

"And Chmara, that's what? Portuguese?"

"Russian," I stammered.

He wanted to know more.

"Because you're Russian?"

I felt infinitely despondent. I was going to have to tell the whole story again, the Revolution, Berlin, Paris, Schiaparelli, America, the Woolworth heiress, the grandmother on Rue Lord-Byron…No. I gagged.

"Are you feeling ill?"

He put a hand on my arm: a paternal gesture.

"Oh, no…It's been ages since I felt this good…"

He appeared to be surprised by my declaration, and all the more so because I'd spoken distinctly for the first time that evening.

"Come on, drink some Mercurey…"

"You know, Unky, you know…" (she paused for a minute and I stiffened, knowing that a lightning bolt was about to strike me), "you know he wears a monocle?"

"Oh, really…? No."

"Put in your monocle and show him…"

She was speaking in a mischievous tone, repeating the words again and again, like a nursery rhyme: "Put in your monocle…Put in your monocle…"

I rummaged in my jacket pocket with a trembling hand and as slowly as a sleepwalker raised the monocle to my left eye. I tried to screw the thing into my eye socket, but my muscles stopped cooperating. The monocle fell out three times in a row. The area around my cheekbone felt paralyzed. On the third attempt, the monocle fell into my peas.

"Well, shit," I growled.

I was starting to lose my composure, and I was afraid I'd blurt out one of those horrible things nobody expects a boy like me to say. But I can't help it, it comes over me sporadically.

"Do you want to try?" I asked the uncle, handing him the monocle.

He got it right the first time, and I heartily congratulated him. It suited him perfectly. He looked like Conrad Veidt in *Nocturno der Liebe.* Yvonne burst out laughing. And so did I. And so did the uncle. We couldn't stop.

"You must come again," he declared. "We have a lot of fun, the three of us. And you, you're quite a comedian."

"That's the truth," Yvonne agreed.

"You too, you're a 'comedian' too," I said.

I would have liked to add, "and a comfort," because his presence, his way of speaking, his gestures shielded me. In that dining room, between him and Yvonne, I had nothing to fear. Nothing. I was invulnerable.

"Do you work a lot?" I ventured to ask.

He lit a cigarette.

"Yes, I do. I have to run this all by myself." He gestured toward the hangar outside the windows.

"Have you been doing it long?"

He handed me his pack of Royales. "I started it with Yvonne's father…"

He was apparently surprised and touched by my attention and my curiosity. He didn't often get asked questions about himself and his work. Yvonne's head was turned, and she was holding out a piece of meat to the dog.

"We bought this from the Farman aircraft company… We became the Hotchkiss dealers for the whole region… We had arrangements with Switzerland for luxury cars…"

He reeled off those statements very quickly and almost in an undertone, as if fearful of being interrupted, but Yvonne wasn't paying him the slightest attention. She was talking to the dog and petting him.

"Things went well here, with her father…"

He dragged on his cigarette, which he held between his thumb and index finger.

"Does this interest you? It's all in the past, all of it…"

"What are you telling him, Unky?"

"I'm talking about starting the garage with your father…"

"But you're boring him…" There was a touch of malice in her voice.

"Not at all," I said. "Not at all. What became of your father?"

The question had slipped out, and there was no taking it back. An embarrassment. I noticed Yvonne was frowning.

"Albert…"

As he said that name, the uncle's eyes glazed over. Then he snorted. "Albert got into some trouble…"

I realized I'd hear no more from him on that subject, and in fact I was surprised he'd confided so much in me already.

"And how about you?" He put a hand on Yvonne's shoulder. "Everything going the way you want?"

"Yes."

The conversation was about to bog down. I decided to mount a charge.

"Do you know she's going to be a movie star?"

"Do you really think so?"

"I'm sure of it."

She blew cigarette smoke in my face, but nicely.

"You know, when she told me she was going to make a film, I didn't believe her. And yet it was true…So your movie's finished, Yvonne?"

"Yes, Unky."

"When can we see it?"

"It's going to come out in three or four months," I declared.

"Will it come here?" He was skeptical.

"Absolutely. It'll be at the Casino cinema." (My tone of voice was increasingly assured.) "You'll see."

"Well then, we'll have to celebrate it. Tell me…Do you think that's a real profession?"

"I certainly do. And in fact, she's going to keep working. She's going to be in another film."

The vehemence of my affirmation surprised even me.

"And she's going to be a star, Monsieur."

"Really?"

"But of course, Monsieur. Ask her."

"Is it true, Yvonne?" There was a little hint of mockery in his voice.

"Yes indeed, everything Victor says is the truth, Unky."

"As you see, Monsieur, I'm right."

This time I adopted an unctuous, parliamentary tone that made me feel ashamed, but the subject was too close to my heart, and if I wanted to talk about it, I had to use any means I could to overcome my elocution problems. I said, "Yvonne has enormous talent, believe me."

She was stroking the dog. The uncle gazed at me, the butt of his Royale stuck in the corner of his mouth. Again, the shadow of anxiety, the preoccupied look.

"And you, you think that's a real profession?"

"The finest profession in the world, Monsieur."

"Well, I hope you make it," he said gravely to Yvonne. "After all, you're no fool…"

"Victor will give me good advice, won't you, Victor?"

She gave me a look both tender and ironic.

"You saw that she won the Houligant Cup, didn't you?" I asked her uncle.

"I was knocked out when I read that in the newspaper." He hesitated a moment. "Tell me, is it important, the Houligant Cup?"

Yvonne sniggered.

"It can serve as a springboard," I declared, wiping my monocle.

He proposed we drink some coffee. I took a seat on the old bluish sofa while he and Yvonne cleared the table.

Yvonne sang to herself as she carried the plates and silverware into the kitchen. Her uncle ran some water. The dog had fallen asleep at my feet. I can still see that dining room in great detail. The walls were covered with wallpaper in three patterns: red roses, ivy, and birds (I'm unable to say whether they were blackbirds or sparrows). The background was beige or white, the wallpaper a little faded. The hanging light fixture — wooden, circular — had ten bulbs with parchment shades. They shed a warm amber light. On the wall, a little unframed picture showed a woodland scene, and I admired the way the painter had profiled the trees against a clear twilight sky, and the patch of sunlight lingering at the foot of a tree. The painting helped to make the atmosphere of the room more peaceful. The uncle, by the phenomenon of contagion that makes you take up a tune you know when you hear it, was singing softly along with Yvonne. I felt great. I would have wanted the evening to go on indefinitely, so that I could sit there for hours and observe their comings and goings, Yvonne's graceful movements, her indolent walk, her uncle's swaying gait. And hear them murmuring the song's refrain, which I dare not sing myself, because it would remind me of that precious moment in my life.

He came and sat beside me on the sofa. Trying to continue the conversation, I pointed to the little picture and said, "Very pretty…"

"It was Yvonne's father who painted that…yes it was…"

The picture must have been hanging in the same place for many years, but he still marveled at the thought that his brother had produced it.

"Albert had a pretty brushstroke...You can see his signature at the bottom, on the right: Albert Jacquet. He was a funny guy, my brother..."

I was about to ask an indiscreet question, but Yvonne came out of the kitchen, carrying the coffee tray. She was smiling. The dog stretched. The uncle coughed but kept the cigarette end in the corner of his mouth. Yvonne squeezed in between me and the arm of the sofa and laid her head on my shoulder. The uncle poured the coffee, all the while clearing his throat with what sounded like a series of roars. He held out a lump of sugar to the dog, who took it delicately between his teeth, and I knew in advance he wouldn't chew up that morsel, he'd suck on it and stare into space. He never chewed his food.

I hadn't noticed a table behind the sofa. On it was a midsized white radio, a model halfway between a standard set and a transistor. The uncle turned a knob, and at once some quiet music came on. We each drank our coffee in little sips. From time to time, the uncle rested his head on the back of the sofa and blew smoke rings. He was quite good at it. Yvonne listened to the music, beating time with one lazy forefinger. We stayed like that, without saying anything, like people who've known one another forever, three people from the same family.

"You should show him the rest of the house," the uncle murmured.

His eyes were closed. Yvonne and I got up. The dog gave us a sly look, got up too, and followed us. We were in the entrance hall, at the foot of the stairs, when Big Ben struck again, but more incoherently and violently this time, so that I imagined a mad pianist pounding the keyboard with his fists and forehead. The terrified dog dashed up the stairs and waited for us at the top. A lightbulb hanging from the ceiling threw a cold yellow light. Yvonne's pink turban and lipstick made her face look even paler. And I, under that light—I felt I'd been submerged in leaden dust. On the right, a mirrored armoire. Yvonne opened the door in front of us. A room whose window overlooked the road, as I could tell from the muffled noise of several passing trucks.

She switched on the bedside lamp. The bed was very narrow. And all that was left of it was the box spring. There were shelves around it, and the ensemble formed a cozy nook. In the left-hand corner, a tiny washbasin with a mirror over it. Against the wall, a white wooden cupboard. She sat on the edge of the box spring and said, "This was my room."

The dog had stationed himself in the middle of a carpet so worn you couldn't make out its pattern anymore. After a moment, he got up and left the room. I scrutinized the walls and inspected the shelves, hoping to discover some vestige of Yvonne's childhood. It was much hotter here than in the other rooms, and she took off her dress. Then she lay across the box spring. She was wearing garters, stockings, a brassiere—all the things women were still encumbering themselves with back then. I opened the white cupboard. Maybe there was something inside.

"What are you looking for?" she asked, propped up on her elbows.

She squinted. I spotted a little schoolbag in the back of the cupboard. I took it out and sat down on the floor with my back against the box spring. She rested her chin in the hollow of my shoulder and breathed on my neck. I opened the schoolbag, slipped a hand inside, and pulled out half of an old pencil with a grayish eraser. A nauseating smell of leather and wax — or so it seemed to me — rose from inside the bag. On the eve of the summer holidays one year, Yvonne had closed it for good.

She turned off the light. By what coincidences and what detours had I come to lie beside her on this box spring, in this small, disused room?

How long did we stay there? Big Ben couldn't be trusted; its chiming grew crazier and crazier, it struck midnight three times in the course of several minutes. I got up and in the semidarkness saw that Yvonne had turned to face the wall. Perhaps she wanted to sleep. The dog was on the landing, in his sphinx position, facing the armoire mirror. He was contemplating himself with bored disdain. When I passed, he didn't flinch. His neck was very straight, his head slightly raised, his ears pricked. When I was halfway down the stairs, I heard him yawn. As before, the bulb shed a cold yellow light that numbed me. Through the half-open door of the dining room I could hear limpid, icy music, the kind you often hear on the radio at night, the kind that brings to mind a deserted airport. Yvonne's uncle was listening to it, sitting in his armchair. When I came in, he turned his head toward me: "Everything all right?"

"How about you?"

"Me, I'm all right," he answered. "And you?"

"Everything's all right."

"We can go on if you want…All right?"

He looked at me, his smile fixed, his eyes heavy, as if a photographer were about to take his picture.

He handed me the pack of Royales. I struck four matches, to no avail. Finally I got a flame, which I very carefully brought closer to the tip of my cigarette. And then I inhaled. I had the sensation that I was smoking for the first time. He was watching me closely and frowning.

"I see you're not a manual worker," he remarked gravely.

"I'm sorry about that."

"Why be sorry, my young friend? You think it's fun to tinker around with engines?"

He looked at his hands.

"It must give you some satisfaction sometimes," I said.

"Oh, yes? Do you really think so?"

"In any case, it's a fine invention, the automobile…"

But he wasn't listening to me anymore. The music had stopped, and the announcer—his intonation was simultaneously English and Swiss, and I wondered what his nationality was—spoke some words I still occasionally repeat aloud, after so many years, when I'm walking by myself: "Ladies and gentlemen, Genève-Musique now ends its broadcast day. Until tomorrow, good night." The uncle made no move to turn the radio off, and since I didn't dare intervene, I heard a continuous crackle of static that eventually sounded like the rustling of the wind in the leaves. And the dining room was invaded by something fresh and green.

"She's a nice girl, Yvonne…"

He blew a fairly successful smoke ring.

"She's a lot more than a nice girl," I answered.

He looked me straight in the eye, with interest, as if I'd just said something of major import.

"What do you say we go for a little walk?" he suggested. "I've got pins and needles in my legs."

He stood up and opened the French window.

"You're not scared?"

He pointed to the hangar, whose contours were shrouded in darkness. At regular intervals, you could make out a bulb, a small point of light.

"This way you'll be able to see the garage."

I'd barely set foot on the edge of that cavernous black space before I inhaled a smell of gasoline, a smell that has always excited me—for reasons I've never been able to identify precisely—a smell as sweet as the smell of ether, or of the silver paper that chocolate bars come in. He took my arm, and we plunged toward the garage's darkest regions.

"Yes...Yvonne's a funny girl..."

He wanted to initiate a conversation. He was circling around a subject close to his heart, one he certainly hadn't discussed with many people. Maybe, in fact, he was bringing it up for the first time.

"Funny, but very lovable," I said.

And in my effort to articulate an intelligible sentence, I produced a very high-pitched voice, an incredibly affected falsetto.

"You see..." He hesitated one final time before he opened up, squeezing my arm. "She's a lot like her father... My brother was so reckless..."

We were walking straight ahead. I gradually got used to the darkness, which was pierced, every twenty meters or so, by a dim lightbulb.

"She's caused me a lot of worry, Yvonne has…"

He lit a cigarette. Suddenly I couldn't see him anymore, and since he'd let go of my arm, I followed the glowing tip of his cigarette. He started to walk faster, and I was afraid I'd lose him altogether.

"I'm telling you all this because you seem to be a gentleman…"

I coughed. I didn't know how to answer him.

"It's obvious you've been brought up well…"

"Oh, no," I said.

He was walking ahead of me, and I tried to keep my eyes on the red tip of his cigarette. There was no lightbulb in this part of the hangar. I stretched my arms out in front of me to keep from banging into a wall.

"This must be the first time Yvonne's met a young man from a good family…" A brief laugh. Then, in a muted voice: "Right, my boy?"

He squeezed my arm very hard, around the biceps. He stood facing me. I could see the phosphorescent tip of his cigarette. We didn't move.

"She's already done so many foolish things…" He sighed. "And now, there's this movie business…"

I couldn't see him, but I'd seldom sensed in anyone so much weariness and resignation.

"It's no use trying to reason with her…She's like her father…Like Albert…"

He pulled me by the arm and we walked on. His hold on my biceps was getting tighter and tighter.

"I'm talking to you about all this because I think you're a nice young man…and well brought up."

The sound of our footsteps echoed throughout that vast space. I couldn't understand how he managed to get his bearings in the dark. If he left me behind, I'd have no chance of finding my way.

"Shall we go back?" I said.

"You see, Yvonne has always wanted to live beyond her means…And it's dangerous…very dangerous…"

He'd released his grip on my arm, but to keep from losing him, I was clutching the bottom of his jacket. He didn't mind.

"When she was sixteen, she figured out some way of buying beauty products by the kilo…"

He accelerated his pace, but I kept hold of his jacket.

"She wasn't interested in spending any time with people from around here…She preferred the summer holidaymakers at the Sporting Club…Like her father…"

Three lightbulbs, all in a row above our heads, dazzled me. He forked left and started stroking the wall with his fingertips. The sharp click of a light switch. Very bright light, all around us. The entire hangar was lit up by floodlights fixed in the roof. The place looked even vaster than before.

"I apologize, my boy, but the only place I can switch on the 'floods' is here…"

We were at the back of the hangar. There were some American cars parked one beside the other, and an old Chausson bus whose tires were all flat. I noticed, to our left, a glassed-in workshop that looked like a greenhouse, and beside it some tubs of green plants arranged in a square. The floor in that space was gravel, and ivy was growing up the wall. There was even an arbor, a garden table, and some garden chairs.

"So what do you think of my open-air café here, eh, my boy?"

We pulled two of the garden chairs up to the table and sat facing each other. He put both his elbows on the table and his chin in the palms of his hands. He looked exhausted.

"This is where I take a break when I'm sick of tinkering around with engines...It's my bower..."

He pointed at the American cars and the Chausson bus behind them. "You see that traveling junkyard?" He made an exasperated gesture, as if shooing away a fly. "It's a terrible thing when you don't love your work anymore..."

I grimaced, or smiled, incredulously. "But surely — "

"How about you? Do you still love your work?"

"Yes," I said, without any notion of what work we were talking about.

"A young man your age is all fire and flame..."

He gave me a look of such tenderness that I was moved.

"All fire and flame," he repeated, mezza voce.

We stayed there, sitting at the garden table, very small in that gigantic hangar. The tubs of plants, the ivy, and the gravel constituted an unexpected oasis. They protected us from the surrounding desolation: the group of waiting automobiles (one of them missing a fender) and the decaying bus behind them. The light from the floodlights was cold but not yellow like the light in the hall Yvonne and I had crossed and on the stairs we'd climbed. No. This light had something gray-blue about it. An icy gray-blue.

"Would you like some mint water? That's all I've got here..."

He went over to the workshop and returned with two glasses, a bottle of mint syrup, and a carafe of water. We clinked glasses.

"There are days, my young friend, when I wonder what the hell I'm doing in this garage..."

He definitely needed to confide in someone that evening.

"It's too big for me..." He swept his arm around, indicating the whole vast hangar.

"First Albert left us...And then my wife...And now Yvonne's gone..."

"But she comes to see you often," I proposed.

"No. Mademoiselle wants to be in the movies...She thinks she's Martine Carol..."

"But she'll be a new Martine Carol," I said stoutly.

"Come on...Don't talk nonsense...She's too lazy..."

A mouthful of mint water had gone down the wrong way and choked him. He started to cough, couldn't stop, and turned scarlet. He was definitely about to suffocate. I pounded him on the back, hard, until his coughing calmed down. He looked up at me, his eyes full of benevolence.

His voice was more muted than ever. Completely worn-out. I understood only every other word, but that was enough for me to surmise the rest.

"You're a nice boy, you really are, my young friend... And polite..."

The sound of a door being closed hard, a very distant sound, but carried by a reverberating echo. It bounced off the back of the hangar. The dining room door, about a hundred meters away from us. I recognized Yvonne's silhouette, her red hair that hung down to the small of her back when she didn't do it up. From where we were, she looked tiny, even Lilliputian. The dog came up to her chest. I'll never forget the vision of that little girl and her giant hound walking toward us, gradually acquiring their true proportions.

"Here she is," her uncle observed. "You won't tell her what I said, will you? That should remain between us."

"Of course I won't..."

We didn't take our eyes off her as she came through the hangar. The dog, on scout duty, led the way.

"She looks really small," I remarked.

"Yes, quite small," the uncle said. "She's a child...a problem child..."

She spotted us and started waving her arms. She called out, "Victor...Victor..." and the echo of that name, which wasn't mine, resounded from one end of the hangar to the other. She joined us and sat at the table, between her uncle and me. She was a little out of breath.

"It's nice of you to come and keep us company," her uncle said. "Do you want some mint water? Cold? With ice?"

He poured each of us another glass. Yvonne smiled at me, and as usual it made me feel a sort of vertigo.

"What were you two talking about?"

"Life," said her uncle.

He lit a Royale, and I knew he'd keep it stuck in the corner of his mouth until it burned his lips.

"He's nice, the count…and very well brought up."

"Oh, yes," Yvonne said. "Victor's a lovely guy."

"Say that again," her uncle said.

"Victor's a lovely guy."

"Do you really think so?" I said, facing each of them in turn. I must have had a weird look on my face, because Yvonne pinched my cheek and said, as if to reassure me, "Yes you are, you're lovely."

Her uncle, for his part, raised the bidding: "Lovely, my boy, lovely…You're lovely…"

"Well, then…"

I stopped there, but I can still remember what I intended to say: "Well, then, may I have your niece's hand in marriage?" It was the perfect moment, I still think so today, to ask to marry her. Yes. I didn't finish my sentence. He went on, in an increasingly hoarse voice: "Lovely, my boy, lovely…lovely…lovely…"

The dog thrust his head through the plants and gazed at us. A new life could have begun that very night. We would never have had to part. I felt so content with her and him, around the garden table, in that big hangar, which has surely been pulled down since.

11.

Time has shrouded all those things in a mist of changing colors: sometimes a pale green, sometimes a slightly pink blue. A mist? No, an indestructible veil that smothers all sound and through which I can see Yvonne and Meinthe but not hear them. I'm afraid their silhouettes may blur and fade in the end, and so, to preserve a little of their reality...

Although Meinthe was some years older than Yvonne, they were both quite young when they met. What brought them together was their shared boredom with small-town life and their plans for the future. They were waiting for the first opportunity to get out of this "hole" (one of Meinthe's expressions), which came alive only in the summer, during the "season." In fact, Meinthe had just become involved with a Belgian baron, a millionaire, who was staying at the Grand Hôtel in Menthon. The baron had fallen in love with him at once, and that doesn't surprise me, because at the age of twenty, Meinthe had a certain physical charm and a talent for amusing people. The Belgian couldn't do without him. Meinthe introduced Yvonne to him as his "little sister."

It was the baron who got them out of their "hole," and they always spoke of him to me with practically filial affection. He owned a big villa in Cap Ferrat and had a suite permanently reserved for him at the Hôtel du Palais in Biarritz, and another at the Beau Rivage in Geneva. A little court, made up of parasites of both sexes, revolved around him and followed him in all his travels.

Meinthe often imitated, for my benefit, the baron's gait. He was nearly six and a half feet tall and walked very fast, with a pronounced stoop. He had some strange habits: for example, in the summer, he wouldn't expose himself to the sun and spent the entire day in his suite at the Hôtel du Palais or in the living room of his villa in Cap Ferrat. The shutters and curtains were closed, the lights were turned on, and he'd oblige some of his ephebes to keep him company. They wound up losing their beautiful suntans.

He was subject to mood swings and wouldn't tolerate contradiction. Suddenly he'd be curt, and the next minute very gentle. He'd say to Meinthe, with a sigh, "At heart, I'm Queen Elisabeth of Belgium...poor, POOR Queen Elisabeth, you know...And I think you understand her tragedy..." From spending time with him, Meinthe learned the names of all the members of the Belgian royal family, and he was capable of scribbling their family tree on the corner of a paper tablecloth in a matter of seconds. He did so several times in my presence, because he knew it amused me.

And thence came his devotion to Queen Astrid.

At that time, the baron was a man of fifty. He had traveled a great deal and knew many interesting and refined people. He often visited his Cap Ferrat neighbor and close friend, the English writer Somerset Maugham. Meinthe remembered a dinner with the baron and Maugham. An unknown, as far as Meinthe was concerned.

Other people, less illustrious but "amusing," assiduously frequented the baron, attracted by his lavish whims. A "gang" had formed, and its members' lives were one eternal holiday. In those days, they used to drive down from the villa in Cap Ferrat, packed into five or six convertibles. They'd go dancing in Juan-les-Pins, or to the Toros de Fuego in Saint-Jean-de-Luz. Only Jacques Fath's or Wladimir Rachewski's "gangs" could rival the baron's.

Yvonne and Meinthe were the youngest members. She was barely sixteen years old, and he was twenty. They were great favorites. I asked them to show me some photos, but neither of them — or so they claimed — had kept any. Furthermore, they didn't much like talking about that time in their lives.

The baron had died in mysterious circumstances. Suicide? Automobile accident? Meinthe had rented an apartment in Geneva. Yvonne lived there. Later she began to work as a model for a Milanese fashion house, but she didn't offer many details in that regard. Had Meinthe gone to medical school in the meantime? He often told me that he "practiced medicine in Geneva," and each time I felt like asking him, "What kind of medicine?" Yvonne was flitting between Rome, Milan, and Switzerland. She was what was called a "flying mannequin." At least, that's what she told me. Had she met Madeja in Rome or in Milan, or in the days of the baron's gang? When I asked her how they'd met, and by what chance he'd chosen her to play a role in *Liebesbriefe auf der Berg*, she dodged my question.

Neither she nor Meinthe ever told me their life story in detail; they dropped vague and contradictory hints instead.

Eventually I was able to identify the Belgian baron who got them out of the provinces and took them to the Côte d'Azur and Biarritz. (They refused to tell me his name. Out of modesty? A wish to muddy the waters?) One day I'll look up all the people who were part of the baron's "gang," and maybe I'll find one who remembers Yvonne...I'll go to Geneva, to Milan. Will I succeed in finding some pieces of the unfinished puzzle they left me?

When I met them, it was the first summer they'd spent in their birthplace in quite a long time, and after all those years of absence, interrupted by brief visits, they felt like strangers there. Yvonne confided to me how surprised she would have been at sixteen had she known that one day she'd be living in the Hermitage and feeling like a stranger in an unfamiliar resort. In the beginning, I was outraged by such talk. As someone who dreamed of having been born in a little provincial town, I couldn't comprehend how you could renounce the scene of your childhood, the streets, the squares, and the houses that made up your native landscape. Your foundation. And how your heart wouldn't beat faster whenever you returned there. I solemnly explained my point of view as a stateless person to Yvonne. She wasn't listening to me. She was lying on the bed in her silk dressing gown, the one with the holes, and smoking Muratti cigarettes. (Because of their name, Muratti, which she found very chic, exotic, and mysterious. That same Italian-Egyptian name made me yawn with boredom, as it resembled my own.) I spoke to her about Route Nationale 201, about Saint-Christophe church, about her uncle's garage.

PATRICK MODIANO

And the Splendid cinema? And Rue Royale, which she must have walked along when she was sixteen, stopping in front of each shop window? And so many other places I didn't know, places that were surely linked in her mind with memories? The train station, for example, or the Casino gardens. She shrugged her shoulders. No. None of that meant anything to her anymore.

However, she did take me several times to a sort of large tearoom. We'd go there at around two o'clock in the afternoon, when the summer vacationers were at the beach or having a siesta. You had to follow the arcades, pass the Taverne, cross a street, follow the arcades again; actually, they ran around two large residential blocks, built at the same time as the Casino, that reminded me of the 1930s apartment buildings on the periphery of the seventeenth arrondissement, along Boulevards Gouvion-Saint-Cyr, Dixmude, de l'Yser, and de la Somme. The place was called the Réganne, and the arcade shaded it from the sun. No terrace, as at the Taverne. You got the feeling that this establishment had had its hour of glory and that the Taverne had supplanted it. We sat at a table in the back. The girl at the cash register, a short-haired brunette named Claude, was a friend of Yvonne's. She came over and joined us. Yvonne asked her for news of people I'd heard her talk about with Meinthe. Yes, Rosy was running the hotel in La Clusaz in place of her father, and Paulo Hervieu worked in antiques. Pimpin Lavorel still drove like a madman. He'd just bought himself a Jaguar. Claude Brun was in Algeria. "Yéyette" had disappeared…

"And how about you? Everything going well in Geneva?" Claude asked her.

"Oh, well, you know…not bad…not bad," answered Yvonne, thinking about something else.

"Are you living at home?"

"No. At the Hermitage."

"At the Hermitage?" She gave a wry smile.

"You'll have to come and see my room," Yvonne proposed. "It's so funny…"

"Oh, yes, I'd love to see it…One evening…"

She had a drink with us. The big room in La Réganne was empty. The sun drew a pattern like wire mesh on the wall. Behind the dark wooden counter was a fresco depicting the lake and the Aravis mountain range.

"There's never anybody here anymore," Yvonne observed.

"Just old people," Claude said. She laughed uneasily.

"A change from the old days, huh?"

Yvonne forced a laugh of her own. Then they both fell silent. Claude considered her fingernails, which were trimmed very short and painted orange. The two of them had nothing more to say to each other. I would have liked to ask them some questions. Who was Rosy? And Paulo Hervieu? How long had they known each other? What was Yvonne like when she was sixteen? And the Réganne, before it was turned into a tearoom? But none of that really interested either of them anymore. As a matter of fact, the only person who cared about their past, the story of two French princesses, was me.

Claude accompanied us to the revolving door, and Yvonne kissed her goodbye and repeated her proposal: "Come to the Hermitage whenever you want...to see the room..."

"All right, one evening I will..."

But she never came.

Except for her uncle and Claude, Yvonne didn't seem to me to have left anything behind in that town, and I was amazed that you could sever your roots so quickly when you were lucky enough to have some somewhere.

The rooms in "palaces" fool you at first, but pretty soon their dreary walls and furniture begin to exude the same sadness as the accommodations in shady hotels. Insipid luxury; sickly-sweet smell in the corridors, which I can't identify but must be the very odor of anxiety, of instability, of exile, of phoniness. A smell that has always accompanied me. In the hotel lobbies where I used to meet my father, with their glass showcases, their mirrors, and their marble, and which are nothing more than waiting rooms. Waiting for what, exactly? The lingering scent of Nansen passports.

But we didn't spend every night at the Hermitage. Two or three times a week, Meinthe asked us to sleep at his place. Those were the evenings when he had to be away, and he charged me with answering his telephone and noting down names and "messages." The first time, he'd made it clear that the telephone was liable to ring at any hour of the night but hadn't offered any clues as to who the mysterious callers might be.

He lived in the house that had belonged to his parents, in the middle of a residential area on the way to Carabacel. You followed Avenue d'Albigny and turned left just past the prefecture. A deserted neighborhood, its streets lined with trees whose branches formed an arch overhead. The houses were villas that varied in size and style according to the fortunes of the local middle-class families that owned them. The Meinthe family villa, at the corner of Avenue Jean-Charcot and Rue Marlioz, was fairly modest compared to the others. Its color was blue-gray, and it had a little veranda overlooking Avenue Jean-Charcot and a bow window on the street side. Two stories, the upper one with a mansard roof and dormer windows. A gravel garden. A wall of unkempt hedges. And on the peeling white wooden gate, Meinthe himself (as he confided to me) had clumsily inscribed, in black paint: VILLA TRISTE.

In fact, the Meinthe villa didn't exactly radiate good cheer. No. Nonetheless, at first I thought the adjective "*triste*" unsuited to the place. Eventually, though, I realized Meinthe had been right, provided you could detect something dulcet and crystalline in the sonority of the word. Upon crossing the villa's threshold, you were pervaded by a limpid melancholy. You entered a zone of calm and silence. The air was lighter. You floated. The furniture had no doubt been scattered abroad. All that remained were a heavy leather sofa whose armrests, I noticed, bore claw marks, and to the left of the sofa, a glass-fronted bookcase. When you sat on the sofa, you were facing the veranda, about five or six meters away. The parquet floor was of light wood but poorly maintained. A ceramic lamp with a yellow shade stood on it, providing the only illu-mination in the spacious room. The telephone was in a neighboring room, which you reached by going along a corridor. The same lack of furniture. A red curtain hid-ing the window. The walls here were ocher in color, like those in the living room. Against the wall, on the right, a camp bed. Hanging at eye level on the opposite wall, a Taride map of French West Africa and a big aerial view of Dakar in a very thin frame. It looked as though it came from a tourist office. The photograph, which was turning brown, must have been about twenty years old. Meinthe told me that his father had worked for a time "in the colo-nies." The telephone was at the foot of the bed. There was a little chandelier with fake candles and fake crystal drop-lets. Meinthe slept in that room, I think.

We would open the French window that gave onto the veranda and lie on the sofa. It had a very particular smell of leather I've encountered only there and in the two arm-chairs that adorned my father's office on Rue Lord-Byron. It was during the time of his trips to Brazzaville, the time of the mysterious and chimerical "African Enterprise Cor-poration," which he created and which I don't know much about. The smell of the sofa, the Taride map of French West Africa, and the aerial shot of Dakar made up a series of coin-cidences. In my mind, Meinthe's house was indissolubly linked to the "African Enterprise Corporation," three words that had lulled my childhood. I reentered the atmosphere of the office on Rue Lord-Byron and rediscovered the fra-grance of leather, the half-light, my father's interminable consultations with very elegant, silver-haired blacks...Was that the reason why, when Yvonne and I spent the night in the living room, I was sure that time had stopped for good?

We were floating. Our gestures were infinitely slow, and when we moved, it was inch by inch. Snail's pace. Any abrupt movement would have broken the charm. We spoke in low voices. The evening invaded the room by way of the veranda, and I could see motes of dust languishing in the air. A cyclist passed. I continued to hear the whirring of his bike for several minutes. He too was advancing inch by inch. He was floating. Everything around us was floating. We wouldn't even turn on the lights as the dark came on. The nearest streetlamp, on Avenue Jean-Charcot, cast a snowy brightness. Never to step out of that villa. Never to leave that room. To stay where we were, lying on the sofa or perhaps on the floor, as we did more and more often. I was surprised to discover in Yvonne such an aptitude for abandon. With me, that corresponded to a horror of movement, an anxiety about everything that won't stand still, everything that passes and changes, the desire to stop walking on shifting sands, to come to rest somewhere, to petrify if necessary. But with her? I think she was simply lazy. Like algae.

Sometimes we even lay down in the hall and stayed there all night long. One evening we crawled into a closet under the stairs leading to the upper floor and found ourselves wedged among indistinct masses that I identified as wicker trunks. No, I'm not dreaming; we did a lot of crawling around. We'd start at opposite ends of the house and crawl toward each other in the dark. You had to creep as silently and slowly as possible to take the other person by surprise.

Once Meinthe didn't return until the following eve-ning. We hadn't budged from the villa. We stayed on the floor, lying alongside the veranda. The dog was asleep in the middle of the sofa. It was a peaceful, sunny after-noon. The leaves were swaying gently on the trees. Far off, some military music. From time to time, a cyclist passed along the avenue with a sound like rustling wings. Soon we couldn't hear any more sounds. They were muffled by a very soft cotton-wool cocoon. Had Meinthe not arrived, I don't think we would have moved for days and days, we would have let ourselves die from hunger and thirst rather than leave the villa. I've never again known moments so full and so slow as those. Opium, it's said, can provide them. I doubt it.

The telephone always rang after midnight, in the old-style, quavering way. A thin, used-up ring. But it was enough to lodge a menace in the air and rend the veil. Yvonne didn't want me to get the phone. "Don't answer it," she'd whis-per. I'd crawl down the corridor, groping my way along, I couldn't find the bedroom door, I'd bang my head against the wall. And having got past the door, I still had to crawl to the telephone with no visible points of reference to help me find it. Before I picked up the receiver, I had a feeling of panic. That voice—it was always the same—terrified me, hard as it was, and yet muffled for one reason or another. Distance? Weather? (Sometimes it sounded like an old recording.) The beginning was invariable: "Hello, Henri Kustiker here...Can you hear me?"

I'd reply, "Yes."

A pause.

"You will please tell the doctor that we'll expect him at nine o'clock tomorrow evening at the Bellevue in Geneva. Do you understand?"

I'd emit a "yes" fainter than the first one. He'd hang up. When he didn't schedule a meeting, he'd leave messages: "Henri Kustiker here…" (A pause.) "You will please tell the doctor that Captain Max and Guérin have arrived. We shall come and see him tomorrow evening…tomorrow evening…"

I wouldn't have the strength to answer him. Anyway, he'd already hung up. "Henri Kustiker" — we asked Meinthe about him several times but never got a reply — became for us a dangerous character; at night we'd hear him prowling around the villa. We had no idea what he looked like, and therefore he became for us more and more of an obsession. I amused myself by terrorizing Yvonne: I'd move away from her in the darkness and announce in my most lugubrious voice, "Henri Kustiker here…Henri Kustiker here…"

She'd scream. And by contagion, fear would seize me too. We'd await with pounding hearts the quavering ring of the telephone. We'd curl up under the camp bed. The phone rang one night, but I didn't manage to pick it up until after several minutes had passed, as in one of those bad dreams where every move you make is as heavy as lead.

"Hello, Henri Kustiker here…"

I couldn't utter a single syllable.

"Hello…Can you hear me…? Can you hear me…?"

We held our breath.

"Henri Kustiker here, can you hear me…?"

The voice grew fainter and fainter.

"Kustiker…Henri Kustiker…Can you hear me…?"

Who was he? Where might he be calling from? Another soft murmur: "…tiker…hear…"

Then nothing. The last thread connecting us to the outside world had just broken. We let ourselves slip back into depths where no one — I hoped — would come to disturb us.

12.

He's on his third "light port." He's not taking his eyes off the big photograph of Hendrickx hanging above the rows of bottles. Hendrickx in his glory days, twenty years before the summer when I got angry watching him dance with Yvonne, on the night of the Cup. Hendrickx young and slim and romantic — a combination of Jean Mermoz and the Duke of Reichstadt. The girl who used to run the refreshment stall at the Sporting Club had shown me that old picture one day when I was asking her some questions about my "rival." Since it was taken, he'd put on a lot of weight.

I imagine Meinthe looking at that historical document for a while and then smiling his unexpected smile, which was never an expression of good humor but rather a nerve discharge. Did he think about the evening when the three of us went to the Sainte-Rose, after the Cup? He must have counted the years: five, ten, twelve…He was obsessed with counting years and days. "In a year and thirty-three days, I'll turn twenty-seven…It's been seven years and five days since Yvonne and I first met…"

The other customer had left, walking unsteadily. He'd paid for his dry martinis but refused to cover the price of the telephone calls and insisted he'd never asked for "Chambéry 233." As the discussion threatened to continue until dawn, Meinthe had told him he'd pay for the calls himself. After all, he explained, it was him, Meinthe, who had asked for Chambéry 233. Him and him alone.

Close to midnight. Meinthe casts a final glance at Hendrickx's photograph and heads for the door of the Cintra. Just as he's about to step out, two men come in, shoving past him with hardly a word of apology. Then three more. Then five. There are more and more of them, and new ones keep arriving. Each of them wears, pinned to the lapel of his coat, a little rectangle of cardboard with INTER-TOURING printed on it. They talk very loud, laugh very hard, give one another heavy slaps on the back. They're attendees at the "convention" the barmaid talked about a little while ago. One of them, more surrounded than the others, is smoking a pipe. They twirl around him and call to him: "President...President...President..." Meinthe tries in vain to make his way through them. They've driven him back almost to the bar. They form compact groups. Meinthe circles around them, looks for an opening, squeezes into it, but once again runs into pressure and loses ground. He's sweating. One of the conventioneers puts a hand on his shoulder, no doubt thinking him a "colleague," and Meinthe is at once absorbed into a group: the "president's." They're pressed together like people in the Chaussée d'Antin métro station at rush hour. The president, who's shorter than the others, protects his pipe by cupping it in the palm of his hand. Meinthe manages to extract himself from this scrum, lowers his shoulder, throws his elbows about, and finally flings himself at the door. He cracks it open and slips into the street. Someone comes out behind him and addresses him: "Where are you going? Are you with Inter-Touring?"

Meinthe doesn't answer.

"You ought to stay. The president's springing for drinks...Come on, stay awhile..."

Meinthe quickens his pace. The other goes on in a pleading voice: "Come on, stay..."

Meinthe walks faster and faster. The other man starts hollering: "The president's going to notice that a guy from Inter-Touring is missing...Come back...Come back..."

His voice rings out in the deserted street.

Now Meinthe finds himself in front of the Casino fountain. In the winter, the jet of water doesn't change color or climb anywhere near as high as it does during the "season." He gazes at it for a moment, then crosses the street and goes up Avenue d'Albigny on the left-hand sidewalk. He walks slowly, zigzagging a little. He looks to be ambling along. From time to time, he gives the bark of a plane tree a little tap. He passes the prefecture. Then, of course, he takes the first street on the left, which is called—if memory serves—Avenue Mac-Croskey. Twelve years ago, that row of new apartment buildings didn't exist. Instead there was a neglected park, in the middle of which stood a big, unoccupied house in Anglo-Norman style. He reaches Carrefour Pelliot. We—Yvonne and I—often used to sit on one of the benches there. He takes Avenue Pierre-Forsans, on the right. I could follow his route with my eyes closed. The neighborhood hasn't changed much. For mysterious reasons, it's been spared. The same villas surrounded by their gardens and their little hedges, the same trees lining each side of the avenues. But the foliage is missing. Winter gives the whole setting a desolate character.

And here we are on Rue Marlioz. The villa is on the corner, down there on the left. I see it. And I see you, walking even more slowly than a little while ago, and lowering your shoulder to push open the wooden gate. You sit on the sofa in the living room, and you haven't turned on the lights. The streetlamp across the way casts its white brightness.

"December 8...A physician in A—, M. René Meinthe, 37, took his own life in his residence sometime between Friday night and Saturday morning. He had, in his despair, turned on the gas."

I was walking along—I no longer remember why—under the arcades in Rue de Castiglione when I read those few lines in an evening newspaper. *Le Dauphiné*, a regional daily, offered more details. Meinthe made the first page, under the headline "Suicide of a Physician in A—." The reader was referred to page six, the page reserved for local news:

December 8. Dr. René Meinthe took his own life last night in his villa at 5 Avenue Jean-Charcot. Mlle. B., the doctor's maid, upon entering the house as she did every morning, was immediately alerted by a smell of gas. It was too late. Dr. Meinthe is said to have left a letter.

He had been seen yesterday evening in the train station, at the moment when the Paris express arrived. According to a witness, he later spent some time at the Cintra on 23 Rue Sommeiller.

Five years ago, after having practiced medicine in Geneva, Dr. René Meinthe returned to A—, the cradle of his family. He was known to have professional problems. Can they explain his desperate act?

He was 37 years old. He was the son of Dr. Henri Meinthe, a hero and martyr of the Resistance, after whom a street in our town is named.

I wandered around and my steps took me to the Place du Carrousel, which I crossed. I entered one of the two little gardens enclosed between the wings of the Louvre Palace, before the Cour Carrée. A mild winter sun was shining down, and children were playing on the sloping lawn beneath the statue of General Lafayette. Meinthe's death would forever leave certain things in the dark. Thus I'd never know who Henri Kustiker was. I repeated the name aloud: Kus-ti-ker, Kus-ti-ker, a name now without meaning, except to me. And to Yvonne. But what had become of her? The words that make us feel another's disappearance more keenly are the passwords that once existed between us and them and have suddenly become empty and useless.

Kustiker…At the time, I formulated all kinds of hypotheses, each one more unlikely than the others, but the truth — I could feel it — had to be pretty bizarre itself. And disturbing. Meinthe would sometimes invite us to tea at the villa. One afternoon around five o'clock, we found ourselves in his living room. We were listening to René's favorite tune, "The Café Mozart Waltz," a record he played over and over again. The doorbell rang. He tried to repress a nervous tic. I saw — and so did Yvonne — two men outside, supporting a third man whose face was covered with blood. They crossed the hall quickly and headed for Meinthe's room. I heard one of them say, "Give him a camphor shot. Otherwise this bitch is liable to croak on us…"

Yes. Yvonne heard the same thing. René came back and asked us to leave at once. He said curtly, "I'll explain later…"

He didn't explain, but a glimpse of the two men had sufficed for me to know that they were either "policemen" or individuals who had some kind of relationship with the police. Certain cross-checks and certain messages that Kustiker left confirmed this opinion. It was the time of the Algerian War, and Geneva, where Meinthe went to his appointments, functioned as a hub. Agents of every kind. Parallel police forces. Secret networks. I never understood any of it. What role did René play in that? On several occasions I could tell he would have loved to confide in me, but doubtless he considered me too young. Or maybe he was simply seized, just as he was about to unburden himself, by an immense weariness and preferred to keep his secrets to himself.

One evening, however, when I kept asking him jokingly who *was* this "Henri Kustiker," and Yvonne was teasing him by repeating the ritual phrase "Hello, Henri Kustiker here…" he looked more tense than usual. He declared hollowly, "If you only knew what those bastards make me do…" And then he added, his voice clipped, "as if I give a damn about their Algerian nonsense…" In the next minute, he'd regained his insouciance and his good humor and suggested that we all go to the Sainte-Rose.

Twelve years later, I realized I didn't know much about René Meinthe, and I reproached myself for my lack of curiosity at the time when I saw him every day. Since then, Meinthe's features — and Yvonne's as well — had grown cloudy, and I felt as though I couldn't make them out anymore except through frosted glass.

Sitting there on that bench in the square, with the newspaper announcing René's death beside me, I saw again some brief sequences from that summer, but they were as blurry as usual. For example, the Saturday evening when we had dinner, Meinthe, Yvonne, and I, in a little eatery by the lake. Around midnight, a group of louts surrounded our table and started yelling at us. Meinthe, with great sangfroid, grabbed a bottle, broke it on the edge of the table, and brandished the jagged neck. "First one that gets close, I slice up his face…"

He spoke those words in a tone of wicked glee that frightened me. And the others too. They backed off. On our way home, René whispered, "Just think, they were afraid of Queen Astrid…"

He particularly admired that queen and always carried a photograph of her. He ended up persuading himself that in a previous life, he'd been the young, beautiful, and unfortunate Queen Astrid. Along with Astrid's photo, he carried the one of the three of us on the evening of the Cup. I've got another, taken on Avenue d'Albigny, with Yvonne holding on to my arm. The dog's beside us, looking very solemn. An engagement photograph, you'd think. And I've kept yet another, much older picture, which Yvonne gave me. It dates from the time of the baron and shows them, Meinthe and her, on a sunny afternoon, sitting on the terrace of the Basque bar in Saint-Jean-de-Luz.

Those are the only clear images. A mist enshrouds all the rest. Lobby and room in the Hermitage. Gardens at the Windsor and the Hotel Alhambra. Villa Triste. The Sainte-Rose. Sporting Club. Casino. Houligant. And the shadows of Kustiker (but who *was* Kustiker?), of Yvonne Jacquet, and of a certain Count Chmara.

13.

That was right around the time when Marilyn Monroe left us. I'd read a great deal about her in the magazines, and I cited her as an example to Yvonne. She too could have a fine film career, if she wanted one. Frankly, she was as attractive as Marilyn Monroe. All she needed was to be as persevering.

She listened to me without saying anything, lying on the bed. I told her about Marilyn Monroe's initial difficulties, her first calendar photos, her first small roles, the steps climbed up one by one. She, Yvonne Jacquet, shouldn't stop along the way. "Flying mannequin." Then her first part, in Rolf Madeja's *Liebesbriefe auf dem Berg*. And she'd just won the Houligant Cup. Each stage had its importance. She must think ahead to the next one. Climb a little higher. A little higher.

She never interrupted me when I was expounding my ideas about her "career." Did she really listen to me? In the beginning, she must have been surprised by such a degree of interest on my part, and flattered when I spoke so ardently about her great future. Perhaps there were some sporadic occasions when she caught my enthusiasm and started dreaming too. But I imagine those didn't last. She was older than me. The more I think about it, the more I tell myself she was living that moment of youth when everything's going to be at the tipping point soon, when it's going to be a little too late for everything. The boat's still at the dock, all you have to do is walk up the gangway, you've got a few minutes left...A soft numbness overcomes you.

Sometimes my little speeches made her laugh. I even saw her shrug when I told her that producers were surely going to notice her performance in *Liebesbriefe auf dem Berg*. No, she didn't believe that. She didn't have the sacred fire. But neither did Marilyn Monroe, in the beginning. Eventually it comes, the sacred fire.

I often wonder where she may have ended up. She's certainly not the same any longer, and I'm obliged to study the photographs in order to recall her face as it was then. I've tried for years without success to see *Liebesbriefe auf dem Berg*. The people I've asked have told me the film doesn't exist. And Rolf Madeja's name didn't mean very much to them. I'm sorry about that. In the movie theater I would have rediscovered her voice, her gestures, and the look in her eyes, just as I knew them. And loved them.

Wherever she may be — very far away, I imagine — does she vaguely remember the plans and dreams I laid out for her in our room at the Hermitage while we were making the dog's dinner? Does she remember America?

Because if we spent days and nights in delicious prostration, that didn't stop me from pondering our future, which I envisioned with greater and greater precision.

I had, in fact, given some serious thought to the marriage of Marilyn Monroe and Arthur Miller, a marriage between a real American girl, sprung from the depths of America, and a Jew. We would have a destiny more or less like theirs, Yvonne and I. She, a little French girl from the country who a few years from now would be a movie star. And I, who would end up as a Jewish writer and wear thick horn-rimmed spectacles.

But France suddenly seemed to me too narrow a territory, where I wouldn't be able to show my true capabilities. What could I hope for in this little country? An antiques business? A rare book dealership? A career as a long-winded, chilly man of letters? None of those professions stirred my enthusiasm. I had to go away and take Yvonne with me.

I wouldn't leave anything behind because I had no ties to anything anywhere, and Yvonne had broken all of hers. We'd have a new life.

Was I inspired by the example of Marilyn Monroe and Arthur Miller? I thought of America immediately. Once we got there, Yvonne would dedicate herself to the cinema. And I'd devote my energies to literature. We'd get married in the big synagogue in Brooklyn. We'd encounter various difficulties. Maybe they'd break us definitively, but if we overcame them, our dream would then take shape. Arthur and Marilyn. Yvonne and Victor.

I foresaw a return to Europe at a much later date. We'd retire to some mountainous region — Ticino or the Engadin. We'd live in an immense chalet, surrounded by a park. A set of shelves would hold Yvonne's Oscars and my honorary doctorate diplomas from Yale and the University of Mexico. We'd have ten Great Danes tasked with mutilating potential visitors, and we'd never see anybody. We'd spend entire days lounging around in our room, as in the days of the Hermitage and Villa Triste.

My inspiration for this second period of our life together was drawn from Paulette Goddard and Erich Maria Remarque.

Or then again, we might stay in America. We'd find a big house in the country. I had been impressed by the title of a book I saw in Meinthe's living room: *Green Grass of Wyoming.* I've never read it, but just repeating "*Green Grass of Wyoming*" gives me a twinge in my heart. When all was said and done, it was in that nonexistent country, in the midst of that tall, translucent green grass, that I would have liked to live with Yvonne.

I reflected for several days on my plan to leave for America before speaking to her about it. There was a chance she wouldn't take me seriously. First of all, I had to settle the practical details. No improvisations. I'd put together the money for the journey. Of the 800,000 francs I'd swindled the Genevois bibliophile out of, I still had about half, but I was counting on another resource: an extremely rare butterfly, pinned to the bottom of a little glass box I'd been carrying around in my luggage for several months. An expert had assured me that the insect was worth "at a minimum" 400,000 francs. It was, therefore, worth twice that, and I could get triple the amount if I sold the butterfly to a collector. I myself would purchase our tickets at the French Line offices, and we'd stay at the Algonquin hotel in New York.

After that, I was counting on my cousin Bella Darvi, who'd made herself a career over there, to introduce us into the film world. And that was it. That was, in broad outline, my plan.

I counted to three and sat on one of the steps of the grand staircase. Looking down through the balusters, I could see the reception desk and the porter, who was talking with a bald individual in a dinner jacket. Surprised, she turned around. She was wearing her green muslin dress and a scarf of the same color.

"So what do you say we go to America?"

I shouted that question for fear it would stick in my throat or turn into a stomach rumble. I took a big, deep breath and repeated, as loudly as before: "What do you say we go to America?"

She came and sat down next to me on the stair and squeezed my arm. "Is something wrong?" she asked me.

"No, not at all. It's very simple...It's very simple, very simple...We're going to America..."

She examined her high-heeled shoes, kissed me on the cheek, and told me I could explain what I meant later. It was past nine o'clock, and Meinthe was waiting for us at the Resserre in Veyrier-du-Lac.

The place reminded me of the inns on the banks of the Marne. The tables were set up on a floating platform, fenced around its perimeter with latticework and tubs of plants and shrubs. Customers dined by candlelight. René had chosen one of the tables closest to the water.

He was wearing his beige shantung suit and waving an arm at us. He had a companion with him, a young man he introduced to us, but I've forgotten his name. We sat across from them.

"It's very pleasant here," I declared, by way of launching the conversation.

"Yes, in a way," René said. "This hotel is more or less a bordello…"

"Since when?" Yvonne asked.

"Since forever, my dear."

She looked back at me and burst out laughing. And then: "Do you know what Victor's proposing? He wants to take me off to America."

"To America?"

He visibly failed to understand.

"Weird idea."

"Yes," I said. "To America."

He gave me a skeptical smile. As far as he was concerned, that notion was just words in the air. He turned to his friend and said, "So are you feeling better?"

The other nodded in reply.

"You have to eat something now."

He spoke to him as though to a child, but the boy must have been a bit older than me. He had blond hair, cut short, an angelic face, and a wrestler's shoulders.

René explained to us that his friend had competed that afternoon for the title of "France's Handsomest Athlete." The contest had taken place at the Casino. He'd been awarded only third place in the "juniors." The boy ran his hand through his hair and addressed me: "I didn't have any luck, none at all."

I was hearing him speak for the first time, and for the first time, I noticed his lavender-blue irises. Still today, I can remember the childish distress in his eyes. Meinthe filled the boy's plate with crudités. He continued to address his remarks to me, and also to Yvonne. He was feeling confident.

"The judges, those bastards...I should have got the top score in free-form posing..."

"Shut up and eat," Meinthe said affectionately.

From our table, you could see the lights of the town in the distance, and if you turned your head slightly, another light, this one very bright, would draw your attention to the other side of the lake, just opposite us: the Sainte-Rose. That night spotlights were sweeping the façades of the Casino and the Sporting Club, and their beams reached the shores of the lake. The water was tinted red and green. I heard a voice, excessively amplified by a loudspeaker, but we were too far away to understand the words. It was a son et lumière show. I'd read in the local papers that the show would feature an actor from the Comédie-Française, Marchat, I believe, reciting Alphonse de Lamartine's poem "Le Lac." I'm sure it was his voice whose reverberations we could hear.

"We should have stayed in town for it," Meinthe said. "I adore son et lumière shows. How about you?"

He was addressing his friend.

"Dunno," the friend replied. He looked even more desperate than he'd looked the moment before.

"We could stop in later," Yvonne suggested with a smile.

"No," Meinthe said. "I have to go to Geneva tonight."

And what was he going to do there? Who would he meet at the Bellevue or the Pavillon Arosa, places Kustiker had mentioned on the telephone? One day he wouldn't come back alive. Geneva, a city sterile in appearance but sordid underneath. A slippery city. A transit point.

"I'm going to stay three or four days," Meinthe said. "I'll call you when I get back."

"But Victor and I will be on our way to America by then," Yvonne declared.

And she laughed. I couldn't understand why she wouldn't take my plan seriously. I felt a dull fury growing inside me.

"The thing is, I'm sick to death of France," I said in a peremptory tone.

"So am I," Meinthe's friend said, in a brutal fashion that contrasted with the timidity and sadness he'd displayed until then.

And that remark lightened the mood.

Meinthe had ordered after-dinner drinks, and we were the only diners left on the floating restaurant. The loudspeakers in the distance were blaring out music that reached us only in snatches.

"There," Meinthe said. "That's the municipal band. They play at all the son et lumière shows." He turned to us. "What are you two doing tonight?"

"Packing our bags for America," I declared curtly.

"He's sticking to his America story," Meinthe said. "So you're going to leave me here all alone?"

"Of course not," I said.

We drank a toast then, all four of us, just like that, not for any reason, but because Meinthe proposed it. His friend ventured a pale half smile, and a furtive flash of gaiety briefly lit up his blue eyes. Yvonne held my hand. The waiters were already starting to clear the tables.

Those are all my memories of that last dinner.

She was listening to me, frowning studiously, lying on the bed in her old dressing gown, the black one with the red dots. I was explaining my plan: the French Line, the Algonquin hotel, and my cousin Bella Darvi...America, in short, the Promised Land we'd set sail for in a few days. And the more I talked, the closer it seemed, until it was almost within reach of my hand. Couldn't we see its lights already, over there, on the other side of the lake?

She interrupted me two or three times to ask questions: "What will we do in America?" "How will we get visas?" "What will we live on?" And so carried away was I by my subject that I barely noticed how much thicker her voice was becoming. Her eyes were half shut, or maybe even closed, and then suddenly she opened them wide and gaped at me with a horrified expression on her face.

No, we couldn't stay in France, in this stifling little country, among these red-faced wine "connoisseurs," these bicycle racers, these gaga gastronomes who could distinguish among various kinds of pears. I was choking with rage. We couldn't stay one more minute in a country where people rode to hounds. Over and out. Never again. The suitcases. Quick.

She'd fallen asleep. Her head had slid down the bars of the headboard. She looked five years younger, with her slightly swollen cheeks, her almost imperceptible smile. She'd fallen asleep the way she used to do while I read her the *History of England*, but even faster this time than when listening to Maurois.

I sat on the windowsill and looked at her. Someone set off a firework somewhere.

I started packing our bags. So as not to wake her up, I'd turned off all the lights in the room, except for the night-light on her bedside table. I took her things and mine from the closets as I went along.

I lined up the suitcases on the floor of the "living room." She owned six, of various sizes. With mine added in, we had eleven, not counting the wardrobe trunk. I gathered together my old newspapers and my clothes, but her things were more difficult to organize, and every time I thought I'd finally finished, I discovered a new dress, a bottle of perfume, or a pile of scarves. The dog sat on the sofa, following my comings and goings with an attentive eye.

I didn't have enough strength left to close the suitcases, and I collapsed on a chair. The dog put his chin on the edge of the sofa and gazed up at me. We stared into the whites of each other's eyes for a good long time.

Dawn was breaking when a faint memory visited me. When had I lived through a moment like this before? I saw the furnished apartments in the sixteenth or seventeenth arrondissement—Rue du Colonel-Moll, Square Villaret-de-Joyeuse, Avenue du Général-Balfourier—where the walls were covered with the same wallpaper as in the rooms at the Hermitage, where the chairs and the beds cast the same pall of desolation over the heart. Drab rooms, precarious stopping places you must always evacuate before the Germans arrive, abodes where you leave no trace.

I slept until she woke me. She was staring at the bulging suitcases. "What'd you do this for?"

She sat on the largest case, the one in dark red leather. She looked exhausted, as if she'd helped me pack our bags all night long. The beach robe she had on was open over her breasts.

So then, keeping my voice low, I talked to her about America again. To my surprise, I heard myself declaiming the sentences rhythmically, and they became a monotonous chant.

When I ran out of arguments, I told her that Maurois himself, the writer she admired, had gone to America in 1940. Maurois.

Maurois.

She nodded and smiled amiably at me. She agreed completely. We would leave as quickly as possible. She didn't want to upset me. But I needed to rest. She stroked my forehead.

I still had so many little details to consider. For example, the dog's visa.

She smiled as she listened to me and never flinched. I spoke for hours and hours, and the same words kept coming back: Algonquin, Brooklyn, the French Line, Zukor, Goldwyn, Warner Bros., Bella Darvi...Yvonne had a lot of patience.

"You ought to get some sleep," she repeated from time to time.

I was waiting. And what could she be doing? She'd promised to meet me at the station a half hour before the arrival of the Paris express. That way, we wouldn't run the risk of missing it. But it had just pulled out of the station. And I was still there on the platform, watching the rhythmic procession of the departing carriages. Behind me, around one of the benches, were my suitcases and my wardrobe trunk, arranged in a semicircle with the trunk standing upright. A harsh light threw shadows on the platform. And I had the empty, dazed feeling that comes over you after the passage of a train.

Deep inside, I'd been expecting it. It would have been incredible had things happened otherwise. I gazed at my baggage again. Three or four hundred kilos I was still hauling around with me. Why? At the thought, an acid laugh shook my sides.

The next train would arrive at six minutes past midnight. I had more than an hour ahead of me, and I walked out of the station, leaving my bags on the platform. Their contents could be of interest to no one. Besides, they were much too heavy to move very far.

I went into the rotunda-shaped café next to the Hôtel Verdun. Was it called the Dials Café, or the Café of the Future? Chess players occupied the tables in the back. A brown wooden door led to a billiards room. The shivering pink light in the café came from neon tubes. I could hear the crack of billiard balls at very long intervals, and the continuous sizzle of the neon. Nothing else. Not a word. Not a sigh. When I ordered some linden-mint tea, I kept my voice low.

America suddenly seemed very far away. Did Albert, Yvonne's father, come here to play billiards? I would have liked to know. A torpor was overcoming me, and I felt in that café the calm I'd known at the Lindens, with Madame Buffaz. By some phenomenon of alternation or cyclothymia, one dream followed another: I no longer imagined myself with Yvonne in America, but in a little provincial town oddly like Bayonne. Yes, we were living on Rue Thiers, and on summer evenings we'd stroll beneath the theater arcades or along the Allées Boufflers. Yvonne would take my arm, and we could hear the *plunk* of tennis balls. On Sunday afternoons, we'd walk around the ramparts and sit on a bench in the public gardens, near the bust of Léon Bonnat. Bayonne, haven of sweetness and rest, after so many years of uncertainty. Maybe it wasn't too late. Bayonne…

I looked for her everywhere. I tried to find her at the Sainte-Rose, among the numerous diners and all the people dancing. It was an evening party that figured in the program of the season's festivities: the "Scintillating Soirée," I believe. Yes, scintillating. Sporadic, brief showers of confetti covered the dancers' hair and shoulders.

At the same table they'd occupied on the night of the Cup, I recognized Fossorié, the Roland-Michels, the brunette, the president of the golf club, and the two sun-tanned blondes. Essentially, they hadn't left their places for a month. Only Fossorié's hairdo had changed: a first wave, glossy with brilliantine, formed a sort of diadem around his forehead. Behind that wave, a trough. And then another, very full wave rose well above his skull and broke in cascades on his neck. No, it's no dream. They stand up and walk to the dance floor. The orchestra plays a pasodoble. They mingle with the other dancers out there, under the showers of confetti. And it all whirls and swirls, wheels and scatters in my memory. All dust.

A hand on my shoulder. The manager of the place, the man named Pulli.

"Are you looking for someone, Monsieur Chmara?"

He speaks in a whisper, close to my ear.

"Mademoiselle Jacquet…Yvonne Jacquet…"

I say her name without much hope. He can't know who she is. So many faces…A steady stream of customers, night after night. If I showed him a photograph, he'd surely recognize her. You should always carry photos of those you love.

"Mademoiselle Jacquet? She just left in the company of Monsieur Daniel Hendrickx…"

"Are you sure of that?"

I must have made a funny face, puffing out my cheeks like a child about to cry, because he took me by the arm.

"Yes. In the company of Monsieur Daniel Hendrickx."

He didn't say "with," but "in the company of," and I recognized in this subtlety a refinement of language characteristic of high society in Cairo and Alexandria, when French was de rigueur there.

"Shall we have a drink, you and I?"

"No, I have a train to catch at six past midnight."

"Well then, I'll drive you to the station, Chmara."

He pulls me by the sleeve. He's acting familiar, but also deferential. We pass through the crowd of dancers. Still the pasodoble. Now there's a steady, blinding downpour of confetti. All around me, a great deal of laughter and movement. I collide with Fossorié. One of the tanned blondes, the one whose name is Meg Devillers, flings her arms around my neck.

"Oh, you...you...you..."

She doesn't want to let me go. I drag her for two or three meters. In the end, I manage to break free. Pulli and I find ourselves at the top of the stairs. Our hair and our jackets are covered with confetti.

"It's the Scintillating Soirée, Chmara." He shrugs his shoulders.

His car is parked in front of the Sainte-Rose, at the side of the lakeshore road. A Simca Chambord, whose passenger door he ceremoniously opens for me.

"Step into my jalopy."

He doesn't start the engine right away.

"I had a big convertible in Cairo."

And then, point-blank: "Your luggage, Chmara?"

"It's at the station."

We'd been rolling along for some minutes when he asked me, "Where are you bound?"

I didn't answer. He slowed down. We weren't going over thirty kilometers an hour. He turned to me and said, "...Travel..."

Then he was silent. Me too.

"One must settle somewhere," he finally said. "Alas..."

We were driving beside the lake. I took a last look at the lights, those of Veyrier on the opposite shore, and the dark mass of Carabacel on the horizon ahead of us. I squinted, trying to see the cable car. But no. We were too far away from it.

"Will you come back here, Chmara?"

"I don't know."

"You're lucky to be leaving. Ah, these mountains..."

He pointed at the saddle of the Aravis mountains, distantly visible in the moonlight.

"They always look as though they're going to fall on you. I'm suffocating here, Chmara."

This revelation came straight from his heart. I was touched, but I didn't have the strength to console him. He was older than I was, after all.

We drove into town on Avenue du Maréchal-Leclerc. Close to the house where Yvonne was born. Pulli was driving dangerously, on the left like the English, but fortunately there was no traffic in the other direction.

"We're early, Chmara."

He'd stopped the Chambord in the station square, in front of the Hôtel Verdun.

We walked through the deserted station hall. Pulli didn't even need to get a platform ticket. My bags were still in the same place.

We sat on the bench. No one else around. There was something tropical about the silence, the warm air, the lighting.

"It's funny," Pulli said. "We could be in the little Ramleh station…"

He offered me a cigarette. We smoked solemnly, without saying anything. I even think I blew a few defiant smoke rings.

"Did Mademoiselle Yvonne Jacquet really leave with Monsieur Daniel Hendrickx?" I asked him in a calm voice.

"But yes. Why?"

He smoothed his black mustache. I suspected that he wanted to tell me something deeply felt and decisive, but it didn't come. His brow was furrowed. Drops of sweat were surely about to run down his temples. He looked at his watch. Two minutes after midnight. Then, with an effort: "I could be your father, Chmara…Listen to me…You have your life ahead of you…You must be brave…"

He turned his head left and right to see if the train was coming.

"Myself, at my age…I avoid looking back at the past…I try to forget Egypt…"

The train was coming into the station. He followed it with his eyes, hypnotized.

He wanted to help me with my luggage. He passed the suitcases to me one by one, and I stacked them in the corridor of the train. One. Then two. Then three.

We had a lot of trouble with the wardrobe trunk. He must have torn a muscle heaving the thing up and pushing it toward me, but he worked in a sort of frenzy.

The guard slammed the doors. I lowered the window and leaned out. Pulli smiled at me.

"Don't forget Egypt, and good luck, old sport."

He said those last two words in English, which surprised me, coming from him. He waved his arms. The train lurched into motion. He suddenly noticed that we'd forgotten one of my suitcases, a round one, by the bench. He grabbed it and started running. He was trying to catch up with my carriage. At last he stopped, panting, and made a broad gesture of helplessness. Then he stood very straight, still holding the suitcase, under the lights of the platform. He looked like a sentinel, getting smaller and smaller. A toy soldier.